Landscape Of Love
BY
Karen Cogan

I0557426

Get Book Three in this series JACK OF HEARTS.

GET TWO FREE SHORT Stories About Grandma Mandy's Early

THE GOLDEN SUMMER

SWEET CHRISTIAN
ROMANCE SHORT
STORY

Years.

CHAPTER ONE

STEPHANIE STEPPED OFF the plane, her heart filled with anticipation as she inhaled the crisp, dry air of the high desert. It was a stark contrast to the sultry humidity of the southeast, where she had spent most of her career. This new beginning, in an entirely different region of the country, promised both a challenge and the opportunity to expand her landscaping skills.

The early spring air still carried a chill, making her shiver slightly as she crossed the tarmac. The terrain in her new home was rugged, the land parched by scarce rainfall, yet bathed in abundant sunshine. The lush ferns and shade-loving plants that had thrived in the east would wither here. Stephanie had devoted herself to studying the indigenous flora, determined to incorporate the beauty of the natural landscape into her upcoming projects.

With a rental car at her disposal, she set out for her new apartment. The Sunday afternoon traffic in this quaint desert town was mercifully light, allowing her a peaceful drive down Main Street. The apartment complex she had chosen stood with its flat-roofed, beige, stucco buildings. She parked outside her ground-floor unit and began carrying in her personal belongings.

Her new apartment welcomed her with low-pile cream carpeting and freshly painted white walls, a blank canvas for her personal touches. The one-bedroom design offered her all the space she needed, fully furnished, sparing her the hassle and expense of moving her mismatched belongings.

Her cell phone rang, the voice of her mother on the other end. "We miss you, sweetheart. It was wonderful having you with us for the last two weeks. The landscaping you did looks magnificent. You truly have a gift, my dear."

Stephanie smiled, grateful for her mother's encouragement. "Thank you, Mom. How are the ferns and spider lilies doing?"

"They love their new home and seem quite content."

Stephanie thought back to how the yard had looked before she arrived to visit her parents during her brief period of unemployment. It had held promise, but it had needed a professional touch to select the right tropical plants to complement the abundant greenery of South Florida.

"When you tire of the browns out there, remember you're welcome to come back here," her mother offered.

"I'll keep that in mind," Stephanie replied, although she didn't say how ready she was to move forward. Her previous employer's retirement due to ill health had brought about the end of her old job.

She had swiftly found an opportunity with Lance Landscape Designs. The owner, Alex Lance, had been impressed with her portfolio and had offered her a chance to plan and oversee landscaping projects in the picturesque setting of the old west. The allure of this romantic adventure had been too tempting to resist, and she even contemplated buying some cowgirl boots and learning to ride a horse.

As the next morning dawned, Stephanie's alarm clock pierced the silence at seven o'clock. Her new work schedule began at eight, but as she wasn't much of a morning person, she hoped to negotiate an eight-thirty start and a half-hour lunch break. After all, her sandwich usually took less than thirty minutes to devour.

"I've got a good feeling about this," she whispered to herself, seeking solace in her morning routine. "There's a reason God opened this door for me."

In a hurry, she donned her azure sweater and pants, then brushed her auburn hair to a glossy finish. With charcoal-gray eyeliner to accentuate her eyes, she felt ready for the day ahead. She would add a touch of rose lipstick after breakfast.

She quickly devoured a bran muffin and sipped her customary cup of coffee before she hopped into her car. As she drove to work, she surveyed the local flora, taking mental notes of Rose of Sharon, English lavender, yucca, and juniper, all common sights in this arid landscape. Their cold hardiness and drought tolerance made them ideal for her designs. She envisioned integrating them with desert favorites like blue fescue.

Upon her arrival at Lance Landscape Design, she parked in the lot, which was adorned with vibrant red lava rocks and strategically placed yucca and blue fescue. The design was visually appealing and resonated with her passion for landscaping.

Checking her reflection in the car's mirror, she smoothed a stray auburn curl and took a deep breath, steeling herself for the new chapter of her life. With a sense of purpose, she headed toward the entrance.

Behind the counter, a woman who appeared to be in her thirties sat surrounded by a plethora of landscaping books. She offered a warm smile as Stephanie introduced herself.

Linda introduced herself with a warm smile, her welcoming presence instantly putting Stephanie at ease. "I'm Linda Lance. Mr. Lance is expecting you. He was impressed with your portfolio,

"I'm excited to be here. I've never worked in the southwest," Stephanie replied, her eyes sparkling with anticipation.

Linda chuckled. "It's the only place I've ever been."

Stephanie said, "I like the landscape. It has character."

"And a lot of prickly pear cactus. Yet, I agree," Linda said with a nod.

Stephanie took a closer look at Linda and asked, "You must be Mr. Lance's wife?"

Linda's eyes widened briefly, registering momentary surprise. She quickly clarified, "No, his wife is deceased. I'm his sister-in-law. I'll call Alex and have him come up."

"Thank you." As the moment to meet her new boss approached, Stephanie's sense of anticipation mixed with a touch of nervousness. She was determined to make a strong first impression. Her desire to succeed propelled her forward.

Soon, a tall, dark-haired man emerged from a door to the right of the reception desk. His striking sky-blue eyes met Stephanie's, and he offered a warm smile as he extended his hand. "Alex Lance. You must be Miss Porter."

Stephanie was slightly taken aback, having expected an older man as her boss. She shook his hand, her gaze locking onto his eyes. "Call me Stephanie. I'm looking forward to working with your team. I've been studying plants native to New Mexico, as well as those that thrive in a dry climate."

"Have you come up with some favorites?" Alex inquired with genuine interest.

"Loads of them. I'm eager to go from looking at photos to using real plants," Stephanie replied in an eager tone.

Alex nodded in approval. "Good. Come on down to our back hallway. I'll show you your office."

With that, Stephanie followed Alex through the door into a short hallway. Her gaze wandered around as he said, "Your office is across from mine for easy conferencing. The restroom is next door to you, and our meeting room is at the end of the hall. None of my other employees have an office here. They're mostly in the field, doing hands-on work implementing our designs."

Stephanie was eager to learn more about her first assignment. "What project are you working on now?"

"The owner of a new shopping center hired us to do the landscape. We also have some jobs for individual clients," Alex explained. "I'm going to have you jump into designing the outside ambiance for a wealthy couple's deck and yard. They want a private, bi-level, paved patio. I put our design catalogs and their phone number on your desk.

Once you are familiar with our style, you can talk to the clients for a better idea of what you should propose. For now, just get settled. Let me know if you have questions."

With a sense of purpose, Stephanie went to her office. On her desk lay a photo of her first project. It depicted a lavish two-story brick house that must be worth a million.

She immediately began envisioning the new deck, thinking of a classic stone with creamy and rosy hues to match the house. Her mind raced with ideas, envisioning a large, concentric circle with raised planters for foliage. Flipping through catalogs, she contemplated colors and varieties of stone.

By late afternoon, she had a sketch of a possible patio to show Alex. She knocked softly on his office door and entered when he invited her in. "I'd like to see if you think they'd like this. I based it on the things you told me they wanted."

Alex held out his hand as she approached, eager to see her work. "Let's take a look."

She handed him the sketch and the catalog pages with materials that she'd marked. Stephanie watched him closely, her stomach fluttering with anticipation.

Alex scrutinized the design, scrunching his eyebrows, and then laid them across his desk for both of them to view.

"I like what you've done with the circular design. The surrounding ledge and fire pit give it closure. Try a water feature on the opposite side of the fire pit. That makes it versatile for winter or summer. The furniture can be moved for a seasonal focus."

Stephanie nodded enthusiastically, taking his suggestions to heart. "I'll work it into the plan."

They continued to collaborate on the design, discussing the choice of foliage like fescue grass, butterfly bush, roses, and other garden plants. "I'll leave it to you to work it into the design," Alex said, appreciating Stephanie's expertise.

Stephanie was still engrossed in her work when Alex left his office at five-thirty.

He poked his head inside her doorway, offering her an option. "You don't have to stay late. I allow my workers to have a life. However, if you do occasionally work late, here's a key to lock up when you leave."

Their fingers brushed as he handed her the key, a small touch that made her feel comforted and less alone in this unfamiliar place. "I won't be much longer. I'm still working on the garden."

Alex gave her a warm smile. "I like your enthusiasm. I'll see you in the morning."

This compliment buoyed Stephanie's spirits. It had been a good first day, and she couldn't wait to share the news with her parents.

In their conversation that night, she conveyed her positive experience, feeling grateful for the opportunity to expand her portfolio of possible landscape designs.

When she went to bed, the unfamiliar surroundings made it difficult to sleep, but exhaustion eventually overcame her. The next morning, she woke up eager to return to work. As she settled into her new role, she couldn't help feeling intrigued by her friendly and intense boss, Alex Lance.

CHAPTER TWO

ALEX WAS SITTING BEHIND his desk when Stephanie arrived. He smiled as he watched her pass his doorway. Her infectious enthusiasm promised to be a valuable asset in working with clients. Not to mention that she was impeccably dressed and strikingly attractive, although, personally, that didn't matter to him. It had been merely two years since Kelly's tragic accident, and he wasn't prepared to open his heart to another chapter of romance.

Deep down, he held strong in his faith in God's sovereignty, and he had turned to Him for solace. The loss of a wife after three blissful years of marriage had left him profoundly scarred. For him, the saying, "It is better to have loved and lost than never to have loved at all," did not hold true. The anguish was too profound, and he knew it would be an extended journey before he dared take the risk of loving again.

The morning was consumed by phone calls and notes on various projects. The crew needed another load of topsoil, and solving other issues occupied the rest of the morning. Just before lunch, he decided to visit Stephanie. She was engrossed with her computer screen and didn't notice him until he spoke.

"How's your day going?"

Stephanie looked up, her brown eyes briefly registering surprise. "It's going well. I'm fine-tuning my plans for the new project. Would you like to see it?"

"I would. You're making progress faster than I expected."

He pulled an extra chair up to her desk, determined to keep their interaction strictly professional. Her lavender-scented hair was a distraction he didn't want to acknowledge. He focused on her design, a two-tier deck with rose bushes at the base. The blend of hardy greens and vibrant colors were aesthetically pleasing.

Turning his attention to the creeping cedar she'd chosen for the border, he commented, "I like it."

He gently tapped her computer screen. "I'd suggest adding another purple plum tree behind the patio to match the two on the sides."

With a swift addition the change was made, and Alex carefully observed the impact. He strived for balance in all his designs, be it in color or composition.

Stephanie sought his opinion, asking, "What do you think?"

"It works. Do you agree, or did you have something else in mind?"

"I prefer it this way. Perhaps a circular bed of tulips and daffodils for a springtime burst of color would be a nice touch. I'll add it and see what you think."

She displayed different arrangements in various groupings and colors until they both settled on a design they found appealing. "When the tulips and daffodils are done blooming, we could have alyssum planted to take their place," she suggested.

Alex nodded in agreement. "That works for me. Will you be ready to present it to the clients by the end of the week?"

"Absolutely. I can get their input and make any final adjustments."

Nodding, Alex pushed his chair back and glanced at his watch, realizing it was nearly noon. "I've noticed you eat lunch at your desk yesterday. I encourage my employees to take a real break. You're welcome to take a walk or do whatever you'd like."

"Maybe I'll take a short walk after I eat. I'm new in town, and don't know any places I want to go."

In a passing thought, he considered inviting her to lunch as a way to get her out of the office. However, it was impractical for several reasons. She might misconstrue his motives. He wasn't seeking a personal relationship, and more importantly, his lunch break was dedicated to spending time with little Daniel.

He appreciated her fervor, and the enthusiasm etched on her face revealed someone who shared his dedication for their work. While he reminded himself that the things he admired about her were purely of business interest, her passion stirred something deep within him.

THE NEXT MORNING, ON her way to work, Stephanie made a pit stop for coffee and a ham and cheese breakfast sandwich.

When she arrived at the office, she greeted Alex, and informed him, "I hope to have the plant selection worked out by this afternoon. I can run it by you if that's convenient."

He looked up from his computer, nodded, and smiled. "That works. I told the client we'd aim to have something for them to review by the end of the week."

"Then I'll get right on it." She turned and unlocked her office door, crossing the sturdy carpet. So far, his suggestions for the patio had been relatively minimal, and she hoped he'd have the same positive response to her landscaping choices.

Throughout the morning, she made the changes Alex had requested. After her lunch, she delved into her favorite part of the project. Her love for plants had been fostered since childhood, and she was enchanted by the opportunity to work with both plants she was already familiar with as well as desert landscaping.

In the late afternoon, Alex dropped by to inquire about her progress. "Do you have the layout ready?"

"I think so. Would you like to take a look? It's still a bit rough."

"Sure, let me see."

He moved over to her desk, and she turned her screen for his inspection. "I like it. The butterfly bush is a nice fit in the large planter. What are you thinking of using in front of the fence?"

"I was considering lavender or cherry sage. I've sketched xeriscaping using white rock, with lavender planted in round beds between the rocks."

Stephanie displayed her ideas on the computer, and Alex nodded in approval. "That looks good. Try a few other plant options and see if lavender still stands out. I need to pick up my son from his sitter. It seems he's come down with a stomach bug. We'll discuss this further tomorrow."

Stephanie was surprised to hear he had a son. From what she knew of him, he would, no doubt, be a dedicated dad.

After her workday ended, she took a moment to chat with Linda. "Alex mentioned that his son is sick. How old is he?"

Linda tilted her head in thought. "Alex?"

"No, his son."

Linda chuckled. "Alex is twenty-seven, and his son is two."

"I hope he's not too sick. It must be hard for Alex to leave work to pick him up."

Linda furrowed her brows. "If his wife, Kelly, were still alive, she would have been the one to get their baby. Unfortunately, she was struck by a car while jogging one evening nearly two years ago and fell into a coma. She never woke up.

Little Daniel was only six months old at the time. Alex was devastated with grief, and my husband and I took care of both of them for a few months. Alex has been coping better lately, but he still misses her terribly."

Stephanie was deeply moved by the tragic story. "It must be incredibly challenging for him to care for a toddler on his own."

"He's fortunate to have a dependable babysitter. She has a couple of preschoolers, and Daniel fits right in like a little brother."

Stephanie nodded. "I should let you get home. You have two school-aged kids, right?"

"Yes. I can't believe how quickly they've grown. They're in the second and fourth grades now. Each night I make dinner and assist with their homework. What are your plans for the evening?"

Stephanie didn't need much time to think before responding, "My life is rather uneventful at the moment. I'll heat up a frozen meal, read for a while, and turn in early. I lived with my parents for the past couple of months, and I miss having someone to talk to in the evenings."

Linda observed Stephanie closely. "There's an older woman named Mandy at our church, whose granddaughter lived with her. A while back, her granddaughter got married and moved out, and Mandy has been feeling lonely without her. She might be open to renting out a room. It could be beneficial for both of you."

The idea of sharing a house was appealing to Stephanie. While she had lived alone in the past, she realized that she didn't enjoy solitude. Her recent time with her parents had reinforced her desire not to spend her life alone.

While she had dreams of finding the right man and starting a family, she held firm to the conviction that he should share her faith and commitment to the Lord. So far, that special person had eluded her. Consequently, someone to keep her company sounded good, though Stephanie doubted this woman wanted a stranger staying in her house.

"Her granddaughter was family. I'm afraid I would be imposing."

"She has some health issues that need watching. It's better if she's not alone. Do you mind if I ask her?"

"No. It's lonely in the apartment, and I'm lucky it's just month to month. Still, I don't plan to move unless she's excited about the idea. I'm a stranger. She may not want me."

"If she's interested, I'll have both of you over for dinner, and you can meet. I'll call her tonight, and let you know what she says."

"Great! Thanks. Maybe it will work out. I certainly could help out around the house."

Linda patted her hand. "That would be so kind.

AS THE BRISK MARCH wind greeted her on her way to the car, Stephanie contemplated her plans for the evening. Reading her daily devotional and finishing her weekly Bible study were high on her list.

She would get started as soon as she fixed supper. Afterwards, she'd enjoy a long soak in the tub while studying her paperback about native southwest plants. There was so much to learn about the region's diverse flora. To unwind, she'd watch one of her favorite comedies and then head to bed. Tomorrow morning, she was determined to resume her jogging routine.

Exercise sharpened her mind and often led to her best creative ideas. Perhaps it would help her complete the first draft of the project that Alex had assigned her. Her heart ached for her boss, and she made a silent vow to offer help if he ever needed it, as a friend, of course.

CHAPTER THREE

THE NEXT MORNING, STEPHANIE stopped at Alex's doorway. Her voice was gentle and filled with genuine concern as she inquired, "How's Daniel feeling?"

He looked up from his desk, a hint of gratitude in his eyes. "Better. He's back with
the sitter today. How are you doing? Do you feel like you're settling in here?"

The sincerity of his interest warmed her. "I do. I love the freedom you've given me to work on the landscapes. That's what I was used to with my old boss. However, I didn't know what to expect here."

Alex leaned back in his chair and steepled his fingers. "I like your work. Keep it up, and I'll sit back and smile."

Her heart ached for him. He didn't smile often, and now, she understood why. He'd been through a lot in the last year. The weight of his personal struggles pressed on her, and she silently vowed to do her best to make his work life a little easier.

"I'll do my best," she assured him, her voice filled with determination. "By the end of today, I can show you the preliminary."

"Wonderful! I'll look forward to it. Let me know if you need anything."

"I will. Thanks."

She headed into her office, clicking on the lights. She made a point of clearing her desk each night. Now, the chestnut surface loomed before her, empty except for her computer. The rest of the room felt equally bare. She had a desk chair, two padded office chairs, and a low wooden file cabinet beside the desk. The room lacked personality.

Her office needed a touch of vibrancy. Tomorrow, she decided she would bring a framed photo of her parents to place on the desk. A trip to a nearby discount store for a small plant stand was also in order. After all, a landscape designer couldn't survive without plants. Once a collection of lush greenery adorned the stand, the office would become more inviting.

While working, she made a mental note to ask Alex for permission to hang some artwork. A few bright prints on the walls would infuse the room with color and create a welcoming atmosphere for clients.

Alex watched Stephanie from his office, appreciating her presence across the hall. He had grown accustomed to working alone in a back hallway, which had been a lonely experience. Now, with Stephanie on board, he was pleased not only with her work but also with her pleasant demeanor.

He had hired her to take on some of the work that had been piling up, and she was proving to be a valuable addition in a very short time. Her smile, which often graced his doorway, brightened up the office.

Her quick adaptation to designing for the southwestern region was impressive. Once she was able to take some of his clients, it would help take the pressure off him, making it easier to balance his work life with the demands of his beloved little son, Daniel.

For Alex, Daniel meant the world. The loss of Kelly had left a gaping void in his life, but Daniel remained a precious reminder of her. However, the demands of parenthood, especially for a toddler, were immense. He hoped Stephanie could provide the support he needed to spend more time with his son.

Alex resisted the urge to let his thoughts wander to Stephanie's bright smile and her attractive features. Love was the last thing on his mind after losing Kelly, and he was determined to focus solely on his role as a father. Maybe, someday in the future, things could change, but for now, his job and his child were his life.

STEPHANIE WORKED DILIGENTLY throughout the day, and by the afternoon, she had completed the project in time to present it to Alex. He studied it closely and then praised her, saying, "You have a good eye for design. How about adding a bench here, facing a semi-circle of roses?"

She envisioned the addition in her mind, appreciating the idea. "That would be a lovely touch," she replied.

He made a few other minor suggestions that wouldn't take long to implement. "Tomorrow, I'll bring the clients in to review your work. Once the project gets started, you'll need to visit the site daily to check on the progress. I love seeing raw earth transformed into a sculpted garden, a place for inspiration, peace, and rest."

With plans set for the next day, Stephanie left the office at the end of the day with a sense of accomplishment. She had secured her first project, and the way forward looked promising.

On her way out, Linda approached her. "Are you still interested in boarding with the older woman I mentioned?"

Stephanie's eyes lit up with anticipation. "Yes, I am. I'd love to meet her and see if it's a good fit."

Linda nodded and continued, "I've spoken to Mandy, and she's eager to meet you. She's been feeling lonely since her granddaughter moved out. Will you be able to come to my house for supper on Saturday night? Mandy will be there."

Stephanie agreed wholeheartedly, grateful for the opportunity to connect with more people. "Yes, I'd love to. What can I bring?"

"I'm baking lasagna, so if you could bring some rolls, that would be wonderful."

"Okay. How many people will be there?"

"Seven adults and three kids. I invited Mandy's granddaughter, Lissa, and her husband, Jason. You'll like them. I also invited Alex and his son, Daniel."

Stephanie smiled her thanks, excited about seeing Alex outside of work and meeting his son. "I'd love to make some friends here. It's a little lonely right now."

Linda smiled at her. "You seem the type to make friends easily. It won't take long."

Stephanie's eyes filled with unbidden tears. "My grandmother helped me make friends when I was going through a rough spot as a kid."

"Were the two of you close?"

Stephanie nodded. "She was there when I needed her. She was my best friend."

Linda reached out to pat her arm. "Is she still living?"

Stephanie shook her head. "She passed away six years ago, but I still miss her every day."

Linda watched her, sympathy brimming from her eyes. "You poor thing. I didn't see either set of my grandparents much. They're retired now. One set lives on the west coast. The other lives in Florida. I hope, when I'm a grandmother, I can stay close to my grandkids."

Stephanie nodded. "I feel the same way."

She got Linda's address and phone number, and then she headed home to the quiet apartment that would be waiting.

She'd often thought about getting a cat. She would have something to greet her when she arrived home. Yet, the apartment she'd rented didn't allow pets. Did Mandy have a pet, maybe a cat, or a nice little dog? The idea of living in a real home with grass and trees appealed to her. She hoped she and Mandy would hit it off when they met.

As Stephanie left, she eagerly awaited Linda's dinner where she might meet her potential future landlord. It wasn't just about finding a place to stay; she longed for companionship in a new town.

THE NEXT DAY, STEPHANIE looked forward to her first client meeting. When Elaine and Richard Pratt arrived, Alex introduced them as the clients that she'd been designing for.. They appeared to be in their early fifties, fit and tanned, with a genuine interest in her designs.

Stephanie invited them to sit, her voice composed yet eager. "Please, have a seat."

They listened attentively as she went over her landscape design, her palms slightly damp as she licked her lips. They examined the layout, sharing glances as they considered their thoughts.

"What do you think?" Elaine inquired, her eyes focused on the plans.

"I like the trees and flowers. The patio looks good," Richard replied, thoughtfully.

Elaine agreed, her eyes sparkling with approval. "I concur, though it's hard to imagine what everything will look like in the end. We were lucky to get in with you so soon. We heard you were booked months in advance."

Stephanie's heart swelled with pride as she acknowledged their good fortune. "You came to us at the perfect time. I just started here and with my arrival, we were able to accommodate new projects like yours."

As the clients examined her design once more, Elaine remarked, "We were fortunate indeed."

Stephanie sighed with relief. It seemed like the project was on track, and she looked forward to helping their dreams of a beautiful sanctuary come true.

Alex, stepping in, sealed the deal professionally, and the couple agreed to start the job the next week. Stephanie admired his skill in managing the clients and securing their trust. As they left to make a down payment for materials, she breathed a sigh of relief. Her first week of work had not only brought in a new project but also the prospect of a new roommate.

Her thoughts soon turned to the upcoming dinner invitation, where she would meet Mandy. The prospect of living in a real home with greenery and companionship was enticing, and she hoped for a positive connection.

THE NEXT AFTERNOON, Stephanie eagerly awaited her first site visit, excited to watch the transformation of raw earth into a beautifully designed garden. Her work and the promise of new friendships infused her life with a sense of purpose.

Stephanie also looked forward to meeting Alex and his son, Daniel, outside of work, as it would offer a glimpse into his personal life and perhaps answer some of the questions she had about her highly disciplined boss.

CHAPTER FOUR

ON THE CRISP SATURDAY evening of the dinner, Stephanie arrived at Linda's house with rolls and honey butter. The moon, shrouded by clouds, cast an ethereal glow, creating a serene atmosphere. The scent of wood smoke wafted through the chilly air, signaling that winter was gradually giving way to the promise of spring as the trees, though currently bare, would soon be adorned with buds.

Stephanie followed the concrete pathway to the front door and rang the bell. Linda promptly answered, and the cheerful light from the foyer spilled out onto the porch. "Come in and let me take your coat," Linda offered warmly.

Inside, Stephanie entered the hallway, her footsteps echoing softly. To the left, a cozy living room beckoned, its ambiance inviting and comforting. Ahead, voices and laughter flowed from a room beyond an arched doorway. Linda hung Stephanie's coat in the hall closet and accepted the food she had brought.

"These look delicious. The butter was a nice touch," Linda commented, her eyes twinkling with appreciation.

"Thanks," Stephanie replied, with a modest smile.

Linda gestured toward the dining room, setting the rolls and honey butter on the table. "I'll introduce you to Mandy."

As Linda led her to the dining room, Stephanie's curiosity piqued. The dining room was separated from the kitchen by a high counter adorned with bar stools, offering an open and welcoming layout. In the center of the room sat a cloth-covered table, already set for the evening. Stephanie surmised that the gracious older woman sitting at the end of the table was Mandy, the woman whom Linda had mentioned.

On the side of the table sat a young couple, sipping a warm drink. Linda paused to make introductions. "This is Mandy, her granddaughter, Lissa, and Lissa's husband, Jason."

Mandy leaned forward and shared a tidbit about the young couple. "They've only been married a year. They just got back from a belated trip to Italy."

Stephanie, captivated by the idea of Italy, couldn't help but exclaim, "Italy? I'm jealous. It must have been beautiful."

Lissa, exchanging a loving glance with her husband, nodded in agreement. "It was."

Stephanie turned her attention to Mandy. "I've been looking forward to meeting you. Outside of work, my best friends are the Wal-Mart greeters."

Mandy chuckled warmly and patted the chair across from Lissa and Jason, inviting Stephanie to sit. As Stephanie settled into the chair, Linda asked her if she'd like a cup of tea. "I have chamomile or peppermint."

"I'd like peppermint, please. I can help you get it," Stephanie offered.

Linda shook her head, declining her assistance. "You sit down and get acquainted."

Mandy, an embodiment of grandmotherly warmth, smiled at Stephanie as she asked Stephanie about her experience working with Alex's company. Stephanie explained her journey from the East and her positive impression of the people she had encountered in the Southwest. As they spoke, Mandy's gray-green eyes sparkled with wisdom, her wavy gray curls catching the warm lamplight.

Lissa and Jason observed Stephanie with curious glances, perhaps considering her as a potential roommate for Mandy.

Mandy shifted the topic to Alex, "I'm so glad he decided to hire you. He was working too hard, and Daniel needed him at home more."

Stephanie, eager to share her observations, praised Alex as a loving father. "I can tell he loves his son. He's a good father, isn't he?"

Mandy nodded with a tender smile. "He's crazy about Daniel. Still, he had a tough time for a while. Jason and Alex have been friends for several years and Jason helped him get through his loss."

"It was a bad time in his life," Jason added, offering his perspective. "It was his faith in the Lord that carried him through."

Lissa, too, affirmed their shared faith. "He's a strong believer."

Eager to share her own beliefs, Stephanie chimed in. "I'm glad to hear he has a strong faith. There are many times I would have been discouraged if I hadn't trusted God."

Stephanie had her own experiences with overcoming adversity, having faced aggressive non-Hodgkin's lymphoma six years ago. With the support of her faith, she had persevered through the grueling chemotherapy, celebrating five years of being cancer-free.

Lissa patted Mandy's hand affectionately. "I was discouraged with life until I came to live with Grandma. She and Jason changed my heart toward God."

Linda returned with a pot of peppermint tea and placed it in front of Stephanie. "Alex and Daniel. Should be here soon. I don't want you to feel like you're still at work, but it's good for Alex to get out. My two kids like to entertain Daniel, so it gives Alex a break."

Stephanie welcomed the idea. "I'm looking forward to meeting Daniel."

In reality, Stephanie was eager to learn more about Alex's personal life. She wanted to see him with his son, hoping it might answer the lingering questions she had about this highly disciplined man.

A few moments later, Alex walked into the room, carrying a child bundled in a soft, warm blanket. He paused in the entryway, gently unwrapping the little boy. As Daniel's hooded coat was removed, he was set free, a burst of youthful energy. Little Daniel immediately ran to Linda, who lovingly scooped him into her arms.

"Hi, honey! Are you cold?" Linda inquired, concern etched on her face.

Daniel shook his head, his big blue eyes sparkling. "No. I hungry."

He turned to look at the dining table, and Stephanie got her first proper look at his small face. He had striking blue eyes like his father, but his hair was a lighter brown than Alex.

Stephanie's heart melted at the sight. This beautiful child had lost his mother, but at least he had Linda as a loving aunt.

Alex removed his coat and hung it beside Daniel's tiny one. As he made his way to the table, his smile enveloped the room, bringing warmth and joy.

Jason stood and shook Alex's hand. "Howdy, stranger. You stay too busy these days for a game of tennis."

Alex nodded, gesturing towards Stephanie. "That's why I hired this lady. She took an entire project and closed it today. I may be back on for an occasional Saturday set with you."

Stephanie hoped with all her heart that she'd never disappoint him.

Alex reached for his son. "Come here, buddy. Aunt Linda's trying to get supper on the table."

Daniel stretched his small arms towards his father, who scooped him up. Just then, Linda's two tow-headed children, a girl, and a younger boy, raced into the room. The girl asked Alex, "May we take Daniel to play?"

"Sure," Alex agreed, gently setting the child down. "You go with Sarah and Allen."

Sarah took his hand and led him down the hallway. Stephanie watched them go, wondering if Daniel would ever have a sibling. Her thoughts were brought back to the present as Alex spoke to her.

"Are you getting to know your potential roommate?"

"Yes," Stephanie replied, her voice filled with warmth. "We're having hot tea together."

"That looks good," he said with a friendly smile. "I'm going to the kitchen to beg a cup."

As he left the room, Lissa chimed in. "Jason and I want to landscape our new yard. Alex has been too overworked for me to ask him to do it. Now that you work for Alex, we may wander in someday to see if you think there's any hope for it."

"I'd love to come up with something you like," Stephanie replied eagerly. "There's nothing more relaxing than an outdoor retreat."

Jason nodded as he placed his hand atop Lissa's, revealing the affection between them. "One day soon you'll look up and see us in your office."

"Good," Stephanie said with a smile. "I'll look forward to it."

Mandy added, "I could use some advice about my yard. My house is old, and my gardens are full of overgrown shrubs. It could use updating."

"I'd be happy to look at it," Stephanie offered. "How long have you lived in your home?"

"About ten years," Mandy replied. "I lived in Houston until then. The house I'm in now has been in my late husband's family forever. I have an extra bedroom since Lissa moved out. I'd welcome a roommate to help around the house in exchange for rent."

Stephanie was pleasantly surprised by the offer. "I'd be happy to do whatever you need, shopping, cleaning, landscape advice."

Mandy gave her a gentle smile. "You're going to be an asset to Alex."

"I hope so," Stephanie said earnestly. "I love the job so far."

Linda brought dinner to the table, and the enticing scent of lasagna filled the room, making Stephanie's mouth water. Linda smiled at her and asked, "I hope you like my lasagna."

The rich scent had Stephanie's stomach rumbling. "Italian is my favorite food. I like all of it."

A blond man with a beard, who had been absent from the room, arrived from the back of the house, carrying Daniel on his shoulders. He introduced himself as Tom, Linda's husband.

The easygoing banter among the family members showed their close-knit bond. Stephanie found herself relaxing and felt more inclined than ever to accept Mandy's offer of lodging. She craved companionship in her new town, and this family seemed like the perfect remedy.

As dinner progressed, Stephanie's heart ached for Daniel, who clung to his father, the only parent he had left. The warm and loving atmosphere of the family gathering made her appreciate the value of such connections.

The evening continued, filled with laughter, good food, and new friendships, as Stephanie embraced her growing connection to the people in this southwestern town.

When Alex left with Daniel, Stephanie was surprised that she missed his presence. Her interactions with the family had been heartwarming, and she was eager to explore the opportunity of moving in with Mandy.

Mandy invited Stephanie to visit her home to consider the offer of free rent in exchange for chores. Stephanie realized that she was seeking companionship and a sense of belonging more than just a place to live. She already liked Mandy and hoped they would become good friends.

THE NEXT MORNING, STEPHANIE looked out at the cold, gray, day, hoping that the upcoming project wouldn't be delayed by bad weather. Her passion for landscaping and her new role in the company had brought a renewed sense of purpose to her life.

At work, she greeted Linda and looked forward to a productive day, working on the landscape project and ordering materials. As she headed to her office with a hot cup of coffee, she passed by Alex's office. He was gazing out of the window, his expression filled with contemplation. Stephanie wondered about his thoughts, whether they were related to his work or his personal life. She knocked gently, and he welcomed her in.

"Good morning, Stephanie. Did you have a good time last night?"

"I did," she replied with a warm smile. "Linda is quite a cook."

"She has some Italian in her background," he explained with a grin.

Stephanie nodded and continued, "I'm ready to start your project. We'll begin prep today, and I'm working on our next project, too."

Alex's gaze locked with hers as he said, "Let me know if you need any help."

She nodded, sensing a growing connection between them, even if it was just a budding friendship. For her, working for the company and getting to know its owner were becoming equally appealing.

Stephanie had observed that Alex was a remarkable man, a dedicated father, and a talented professional. As they each embraced their roles, Stephanie wondered if there might be more to their relationship in the future, even if she wasn't actively seeking it.

CHAPTER FIVE

ALEX STOOD IN FRONT of his building, basking in the warmth of the spring sunshine. He surveyed the landscaping surrounding his business, checking if any updates or plant replacements were needed. The back of the building posed no issues since it shared a concrete parking lot with three neighboring businesses on the corner.

A quick glance assured him that the irrigation system was functioning well for the small bushes, and the bed of petunias promised an early burst of color following the winter's browns. The tulips and daffodils would soon paint the area in vibrant hues. He believed that a successful landscape design depended on the harmonious combination of form and color.

As he entered the office, Linda greeted him, inquiring, "Is everything going smoothly at the site?"

"Yep. Stephanie's got it well under control," he replied.

Linda probed further. "Are you going out for lunch today?"

Alex contemplated the idea for a moment. "No, I'll grab something from the fridge. Working through lunch should help me leave the office on time."

Linda smiled warmly, knowing his motivations. "Good. You'll get to spend more time with Daniel."

Alex's eyes softened at the mention of his son. "He's hardly a baby anymore. I'm surprised by how fast he's growing."

Linda nodded knowingly. "That's why Stephanie is here. You need more time to be a father to him."

Alex returned the smile. "I totally agree."

Stephanie took their attention away from their conversation as she entered Alex's office. She said, "The project is coming along nicely.

They've made satisfactory progress. The ground is ready for laying the patio."

"Let me know when they finish so we can proceed with planting," Alex instructed.

"I'll let you know right away," Stephanie replied, her wind-tousled hair and rosy cheeks enhancing her charm. They were kindred spirits in their love for the outdoors He inquired, "Will you be visiting Mandy's house tonight?"

Stephanie confirmed with a nod. "Yes, she's cooking supper."

Alex knew she was in for a treat. "You'll enjoy it."

"So I've heard. I like Mandy, and her granddaughter seems lovely as well," Stephanie commented.

Alex nodded in agreement. "She is. She's been great for Jason. At first, Mandy was the only one who believed it would work."

Curious, Stephanie inquired. "They must have something in common."

"They always did. It just took them a while to realize it," Alex revealed.

"And now, it's happily ever after," Stephanie observed.

A shadow crossed Alex's face, and he admitted with a hint of pain, "I hope so. It doesn't always work that way."

Feeling sympathetic, Stephanie hastily added, "I'm sorry. There' is no guarantee. It didn't work that way for you."

Alex managed a sad smile. "No, it didn't."

Embarrassed by her inadvertently blunt remark, Stephanie whispered, "I'm sorry. I should have been more considerate. I didn't mean to bring up any painful memories."

Alex's gentle hand on her shoulder caught her off-guard. "Don't worry about it. I've learned not to hold grudges against the happiness of others."

"That's commendable. Sometimes, it's a struggle for me to be that way," Stephanie confessed.

Alex opened up. "It's not easy, but it's the right path. And, yes, it's faith that helped me through the darkest days after Kelly's death."

Stephanie nodded, understanding his journey. "It's a testament to your strength."

"I appreciate your understanding, Stephanie. Now, I suppose we should get back to work."

She left his office, determined to focus on her tasks. Yet, her thoughts kept circling back to the haunting eyes of a man who had endured so much.

THE NEXT MORNING, STEPHANIE told Linda about her evening with Mandy.

" I knew you'd enjoy your visit," Linda replied.

"Yes and she invited me back tonight."

They talked about Mandy for a minute longer before Stephanie walked to her office and found a note from Alex on her desk. He needed her to create a time projection for a project they were working on. Stephanie turned on her computer, opened her design software, and began her task. The project was her main focus for most of the morning.

After lunch, Alex returned to the office and stopped by Stephanie's desk to review her work. He appreciated her efforts and suggested, "Maybe you could deliver this projection to the site this afternoon."

"Certainly. I'd welcome a change of scenery," she responded with a hint of eagerness. Wanting to know more about Alex's new venture, she asked, "How is your new job going?"

Alex leaned against her desk, sharing the details. "Quite well. I've estimated a six-month completion timeline for the new project at the sports complex for the city. It's not my first time working with them. I previously did a project for the city office complex."

Piquing her interest, Stephanie offered, "I have an idea. Maybe I can help you expand into southern Colorado. With a little advertising, I think we could pick up some jobs there."

Alex contemplated her suggestion. "We're doing well here. Expanding might be a bit challenging, especially with the current workforce. However, if you're up for taking an extra job every few weeks and exploring new areas in Colorado, it could be a worthwhile venture."

Thrilled with his encouraging response, Stephanie beamed. "I'd love the challenge, and it's an excellent opportunity for growth."

Alex smiled back, indicating his trust in her. "You might even help turn this business into a multi-million-dollar company someday."

She marveled at the possibilities. "I'll research advertising options and get back to you soon."

Alex was open to her input. "Sounds good. Let me know when you have some ideas."

As Stephanie watched him walk away, she noticed how attractive he was. His soulful blue eyes had a way of leaving a lasting impression. She pondered the idea of him smiling at her with affection, but quickly shook off her thoughts. She was sure he wasn't looking for love, and she needed to focus on her career.

Stephanie continued her work with renewed determination. Nonetheless, her thoughts turned to Kelly, the woman Alex had lost. Linda had shared that Kelly had worked in the office before becoming a mother. Stephanie wondered what the person had been like who had left a void in Alex's life.

As the day passed, Stephanie's excitement mounted about moving in with Mandy. When she finished work, her stroll to her car through the cool spring night brought a sense of anticipation,. She noticed the blossoming buds and new green leaves on the trees all around her. Living close to southern Colorado meant that next winter, she would have probably have the chance to experience snow. Perhaps she would even try her hand at skiing.

She knocked on Mandy's door. The petite woman with gray-green eyes and a bright smile greeted her. "Come in, dear. I've been looking forward to this all day."

Stephanie entered. She inhaled the homey scent of the dinner Mandy was cooking. It brought back childhood memories of coming home from school to her mother's meals.

Nostalgia engulfed her.

She followed Mandy into the parlor. Creamy lace sheers covered the front window. The room also held a claw-legged floral sofa with doilies on the armrests. Cystal lamps with powder-blue shades and fringe sat atop the reddish-brown end tables, polished and shiny like the coffee table.

"Sit down," Mandy invited. "I'll get us some tea and be right back. I want to hear how your job is going."

Moments later, Mandy brought in two tall glasses. Condensed water droplets rolled down the sides. Stephanie thanked Mandy and accepted one. As she sipped it, she noticed it wasn't as sweet as she was used to. Still, it was brisk and refreshing.

"Your house is lovely. I already feel at home."

Mandy smiled. A dimple showed on her cheek. "I'm glad you like it. Fortunately, it's cozy in the winter. I like to open these curtains and watch the snow fall." She gestured to the window behind the sofa.

Continuing, she said, "It's not a large house. Although, after I got used to Lissa's company, it seemed too big to ramble around in all by myself. It's too quiet."

Stephanie nodded. "I know what you mean. I've lived by myself in apartments for the last few years. There's no one to talk to about your day when you get home from work."

"Lissa used to do that when she came home."

"You miss her a lot, don't you?"

Mandy cocked her head thoughtfully. "I do. Yet, I couldn't be more delighted that she has the kindest, gentlest husband I could wish for her."

"She's very blessed. That kind of man can be hard to find. I know because I've looked."

"That's what Lissa said when she came here. Don't give up. He's out there somewhere."

Stephanie warmed to the older woman's encouragement. She'd heard Mandy was a strong believer. It would be uplifting to share a house with another Christian. So often, in day-to-day living, Stephanie forgot to include God in her thoughts and actions. Perhaps Mandy's strong faith would impact Stephanie's daily walk with God..

Stephanie's stomach rumbled as a timer went off in the kitchen, focusing her attention on the heady scent drifting into the parlor.

Mandy stood, saying, "Dinner's ready. Come on and let's eat."

Following along the archway from the parlor to the dining room, Stephanie ran her finger along the edge of the polished wooden table. This is beautiful."

"My husband carved it. Though he was a mechanic, he loved to work with wood."

"He was talented."

Mandy smiled. "Yes, he was."

As they entered the kitchen, Mandy said, "Now, you sit down right here and have a taste of this meatloaf and mashed potatoes. I've got some fresh green beans and rolls. There's peach cobbler for dessert."

"You've gone to too much trouble. I could have brought something to save you work."

"Nonsense. I love to cook hearty meals. I just need someone to share them with me."

As Mandy arranged the bowls and platters on the table, her look of pleasure told Stephanie that Mandy found purpose in her task. If that were the case, Stephanie would insist on pitching in on grocery money and enjoying the benefits.

"We'll have a blessing and dig right in," Mandy said. She cleared her throat and began. "Dear Lord, we thank you for providing for us. We know every good gift comes from You. Thank You for this food and we pray that its nourishment will fuel us for Your service. Amen."

Stephanie echoed "Amen," and Mandy handed her the spatula.

She lifted out a slice of meatloaf and surrounded it with potatoes and beans. After one taste of each, she was hooked. "This is delicious!"

Mandy beamed. "Thank you. What are your favorite foods?"

Stephanie chuckled. "Most anything that doesn't come from a can. For my birthday, I always asked for fried chicken, mashed potatoes, and corn. I've never been a picky eater, though."

"That's good. If you decide to live here, I won't have to worry about making things you don't like."

Stephanie realized she'd already decided if Mandy have her, she would happily accept. This dwelling was an oasis of peace and serenity. "I definitely want to live here. You tell me what chores need to be done each week, and I'll tend to them."

Mandy poured more tea into the glasses. "You've seen my house and know that it's small but cozy."

"Yes. I love it. I'd like to see my room again when we finish eating."

"We'll take another tour after supper."

When they'd finished the main course, they held off on the cobbler to show Stephanie her bedroom again. Mandy led the way down the bedroom hallway lined with photos of her son and late husband. They were smiling, having an enjoyable time when the camera caught them.

Nostalgia at how quickly the years passed bored into Stephanie's mind. Mandy had been a young mother in several of these shots. Now she was a widow and a great-grandmother. Stephanie hoped, like Mandy, that she might touch others with her life.

The bedroom charmed Stephanie again with blue flowered wallpaper, a white chenille bedspread, and billowy blue valances above cream-colored shades. The maple headboard matched the dresser and chest. It wasn't a large room, but it was a cozy nest.

They peeked into Mandy's floral décor bedroom and last of all, the garage, which housed the washer and dryer. The convenience was undeniable. When they got back to the kitchen, Mandy served the cobbler with a scoop of ice cream on top.

After a bite, Stephanie said, "I'm sold. When can I move in?"

Grandma Mandy smiled. "Any time you like. Do you have a lease on your apartment?"

"Six months," Stephanie answered, "But I'm sure I can break it. Rentals are in short supply here, aren't they?"

Grandma Mandy nodded. "Yes. I doubt you'll have any trouble."

Stephanie looked forward to settling in with Mandy, and she asked, "How about next week? Is that too soon?"

Mandy shook her head. "Absolutely not. I'll have your room clean and ready."

Stephanie doubted there'd be any more cleaning the room could need. It looked spotless already, as did the rest of the house. "Please don't go to all that trouble. It looked beautiful and I can do any cleaning needed after I get settled."

"It's no trouble. I'll launder the bedding and curtains, vacuum, and dust. I want it to be nice for you. I have to do those things anyway, you know."

Stephanie made an inner promise that it wouldn't be that way after she lived here. She'd take over the heavier chores, such as vacuuming and scrubbing, leaving Mandy to putter in the kitchen. She had heard that Mandy had a heart attack several months earlier and needed to spend her time on strolls around the neighborhood and doing church activities that she enjoyed.

After the last bite of the cobbler, Stephanie told Mandy, "I won't feel right unless you let me help clean up the dishes. Besides, I need to learn where things go."

She was relieved when Mandy agreed. "All right. I'll show you where I store what we'll use."

While they puttered together putting away the leftovers, they shared stories about their lives. Mandy described her countrified childhood and Stephanie shared her interest in landscape design.

The time passed swiftly. When they finished, Stephanie felt she'd known Mandy for years. When she said good night, she was looking forward to moving into the cozy house and sharing it with her new friend.

When she returned to her apartment, the loneliness weighed heavy on her. The thought of Mandy's warm and welcoming home offered the comfort she longed for. Stephanie prepared for bed, wrapped in her solitude, and drifted to sleep after saying a prayer of thanks to God for her new friend..

THE FOLLOWING MORNING, Linda asked her about her visit with Mandy. Stephanie beamed with excitement. "It was great, and I've decided to move in as soon as I can."

Linda nodded, pleased by her enthusiasm. "I knew you'd like it there."

The promise of moving in with Mandy brought a sense of joy and contentment. It was an opportunity to share her life with someone she already considered a dear friend.

CHAPTER SIX

ALEX'S FACE LIT UP with a bright, hopeful grin as he strolled to his office. In his mind's eye, he envisioned a burgeoning web of contracts, woven across the local area. With Stephanie at his side, he felt confident that they made a formidable team. Their collaboration held the potential to breathe new life into his company.

However, beneath the surface of excitement, a gnawing doubt lingered. He couldn't let himself become too reliant on Stephanie. She was, after all, an employee. People could leave, just as Kelly had left his life, leaving a void that time had yet to fully heal. He had learned the painful lesson of losing someone dear, and he was reluctant to tread that path again, even if it were only a valued employee who might depart.

Nevertheless, Stephanie's unwavering enthusiasm was infectious. She had a knack for spotting opportunities that had eluded him. The idea of expanding into southern Colorado, for instance, was a concept he wouldn't have thought about doing. It was almost as if she was a breath of fresh air, a welcome presence, perhaps even a guiding hand sent the Almighty to open his eyes to uncharted territories.

Later in the afternoon, his day took an unexpected turn as a call came in from Daniel's babysitter, reporting her illness. This posed an urgent dilemma. The sitter had agreed to look after Daniel through the evening so that Alex could attend a crucial business dinner with a corporate client. The client's schedule had been challenging to align with, and canceling the meeting could hinder the progress of the ongoing job.

Frustrated after a couple of unsuccessful calls for help, he decided to seek assistance from Linda. However, she was volunteering at her children's school during their Open House that night. His options dwindling, Alex pondered his next move and reached out to Mandy, but she had a Bible study meeting scheduled at her house for the evening.

Just when the predicament seemed insurmountable, Stephanie, who had been eavesdropping on the conversation, chimed in with a surprising offer. "It sounds like you need a sitter for Daniel. I can help you with that, if you like."

Taken aback, Alex considered her proposal. Babysitting his child was certainly not within her job description, and he was hesitant to impose on her.

"I would never ask you to do that," he replied with a touch of uncertainty.

Stephanie's sincerity shone through as she asserted, "You didn't. I offered. He's an adorable little boy, and I'd genuinely enjoy his company."

Alex, touched by her generosity, contemplated whether or not to accept her offer. Finally, he replied, "I would pay you for your time, commensurate with your salary, as this is related to business."

Stephanie frowned at the idea of payment. Her response was genuine as she said, "Absolutely not. This is something I want to do."

Satisfied with her intentions, Alex felt a weight lift off his shoulders. He recognized Stephanie's kindness and dedication, and while he was sure she would protest, he decided to find a way to express his gratitude, perhaps by inviting her to a nice dinner as a token of appreciation. Naturally, he intended to word the invitation in a way that conveyed his gratitude without any romantic overtures. Out of loyalty to Kelly, he had shut the door on his own romantic inclinations, and between his responsibilities as a single parent and his demanding work, he hadn't felt the pull of attraction in a long time.

However, Stephanie's warmth and compassion made him question if he had simply not yet met the right woman.

Setting his feelings aside, he rushed to pick up Daniel and return home. Soon after, Stephanie arrived, looking casual and comfortable in soft, pink cardigan and beige slacks. Her presence brought a flicker of curiosity to Alex about how she maintained such an appealing appearance.

As she approached Daniel, she spoke with gentle reassurance. "Hi, honey. I'm going to stay with you while your daddy goes out. We'll have fun, and then he'll come back."

The child, with solemn blue eyes, stared at her and tentatively sucked his thumb. Puzzled, he raised his arms towards Alex. Stephanie rose to let Alex introduce them.

Gently, he explained, "This is Stephanie. She's a nice lady who wants to play with you. I promise you'll like her."

Although Daniel continued to regard Stephanie with an intense and unrelenting gaze, he did not burst into tears, as she had feared. His tiny lip quivered for a moment as he stared at the closed door when Alex left.

Extending her hand, Stephanie asked, "Will you show me your room?"

With only a brief hesitation, Daniel took her hand and led her down the hallway into a room strewn with colorful toys. It was evident that he had been amusing himself while his father prepared for the dinner meeting.

Lifting a plastic dinosaur, Daniel waved it in the air, mimicking a roar. Stephanie smiled and sat down near the doorway. She happily entered his world. When Daniel placed the dinosaur in her lap, she engaged Daniel by pretending that it was flying.

Laughter filled the room as they played together. Soon, the dinosaurs became involved in epic battles, and Daniel playfully growled and collided the plastic creatures until one emerged victorious. Stephanie marveled at the simple joys of a child's imagination.

When the doorbell rang, Stephanie accepted the pizza delivery, and the child followed her to the kitchen.

She set the box on the table, washed Daniel's hands, and lifted him into a booster chair. Setting a slice before him, she asked, "What would you like to drink?"

"Mik," came the immediate reply.

She poured milk into a lidded cup she found in the pantry and set it on the table. Getting herself a soda and slice of pizza, she sat next to him and said a prayer for their food. He grinned at her happily, a slice of pepperoni halfway in his mouth.

They enjoyed their pizza together, and the little boy's enthusiasm was contagious.

After finishing dinner, he munched on two cookies. With his appetite sated, he approached her with a sense of adventure in his eyes. He tugged at her hand, asking to play again. She gladly accepted his invitation, and they returned to his room.

Despite initially playing with his dinosaur collection, he eventually reached into his toy chest and retrieved a well-loved, brown rabbit.

Daniel rubbed his nose in the worn fur. "Squeaky."

"Squeaky?" she asked, thinking it sounded like a name for a mouse. Daniel set the rabbit on his toddler bed.

"Does Squeaky sleep with you?" Stephanie asked.

Nodding, Daniel wandered to a set of blocks sitting in a plastic crate. He threw them out in handfuls before squatting down to build.

Stephanie sat down beside him and assembled a flat-roofed house. Daniel stuck his foot into it and knocked it over, giggling at the result. Stephanie constructed a block tower, and he knocked it down. From then on, the game was strictly demolition.

Ten minutes later, he'd wandered off to jump on a tiny toddler trampoline. Stephanie picked up the blocks and then watched his energetic performance.

When he was finally tired out, he was content to sit in her lap for a story. At eight-thirty, she put on his pajamas and brushed his teeth.

"Time for bed, Tiger," she said.

She expected a protest. Instead, he stuck his thumb in his mouth and allowed her to lead him back into the bedroom. She lifted him into bed. "Do you want to sleep with Squeaky?"

He nodded, and she handed him the rabbit. He snuggled in, holding it near his face. He pointed to a rocket ship nightlight plugged into an outlet. "Little light," he said.

"I'll turn it on," Stephanie promised.

On the way out, she flipped it on and turned off the overhead light. He didn't make a peep. When she checked on him ten minutes later, he was asleep.

Returning to the living room, Stephanie settled on the sofa, and became engrossed in a novel until Alex returned. A blustery breeze followed him inside, making her shiver. His sigh bespoke his weariness.

"How did Daniel do?" he asked.

She gazed into his eyes. "Wonderfully! We ate pizza and played in his room. We had a terrific time."

"That's a relief. You put in a long day. You didn't deserve an exhausting evening."

"It was fun, and I was impressed at how well he went to bed. Back in my distant babysitting days, that was usually the hardest part of the evening."

Alex settled on the other end of the couch. "I enjoy his company, yet there are nights I'm glad to see him go to sleep."

"I bet all honest parents would say that," she said.

"I hope so. I try to be with him as much as I can."

Knowing it must be hard to be mother and father to the little boy, Stephanie said, "He knows how much you love him. That's why he's so secure."

Alex smiled at her. "You're good for my parenting esteem. Listen, I was wondering if I could take you to dinner soon to thank you for filling in for me tonight? I thought about bringing you back a dessert, but I didn't know what you'd like."

It struck her as a sweet thought. Dinner would be more intimate than anything they'd done. She felt sure he didn't mean it as a date. Should she risk outside of work time with him? She found him far too attractive as it was.

"I was happy to do this. You don't need to take me to dinner."

"I want to. We can talk about the job you're working on."

She nodded, feeling a stab of disappointment. What else would they talk about? She hadn't wanted it to be personal, had she?

"That would be nice, then," she said. "Let me know what time."

He nodded. "We'll touch base tomorrow at the office and decide on a good time."

"All right. How did your corporate dinner go? Was he interested in hiring the firm?"

Lines of weariness lifted from his face when he answered. "We got along really well. He liked our ideas. We have an informal agreement. He's coming in to sign the contract tomorrow."

"That's wonderful! It's going to keep you busy."

"It will keep us both busy. I'm going to need your help. He wants the design drawn in two weeks and to have the contractor start a week after that. Everything must be in place by the opening of the shopping center."

Stephanie fingered the lacy cuff on her blouse. "That's a tight deadline. We still have two jobs in progress. I hope nothing goes wrong with those."

"I'm praying everything will go smoothly. Even if it doesn't, we'll work on one problem at a time. We have a good crew working on the one you're managing."

Stephanie agreed. "It's nearly two-thirds complete. The grass is laid, and the carpenter is nearly finished with his part. I was at the site yesterday and we're meeting the schedule, though there are still things to do. Speaking of things to do, I should get going. I'm packed to move to Mandy's house and want to see if I missed anything."

"She's such a nice lady. You will enjoy being with her."

Smiling back, she said, "I already do."

When she'd gathered her purse and book, she headed for the door. "I'll have the project ready for you to look at in the morning. I'm glad your meeting went well tonight."

He smiled at her. "Thanks to you. Have a good evening."

"You, too." She took the memory of his smile with her as she trod into the still, cool evening. Stars filled the sky with a thousand lights. No landscaping she could ever attempt would compare with the beauty of what God had already created. She was blessed to view what He provided.

Upon her return to her apartment, she walked around the boxes she had packed and set aside, a reminder of her upcoming move to Mandy's house. Sharing a home with a warm and gracious companion was a concept she hadn't experienced before, and it filled her with anticipation. Her solitude was soon to be replaced with the promise of a cherished friendship, a change that brought comfort and happiness.

The following morning, she wrapped herself in a cozy sweater to fend off the lingering chill of the early spring air. As she left her apartment, she felt a hint of excitement about the day ahead. The promise of seeing Alex again added an extra layer of anticipation to her arrival at work.

Chapter Seven

LINDA NODDED AS STEPHANIE entered the building. Linda's expression was tinged with concern. "Alex is on the phone with one of the contractors, and things don't sound good. You might want to leave him alone to work it out."

Stephanie furrowed her brows, a hint of worry in her eyes. "Really? I've never seen him upset."

Linda nodded and offered a knowing smile. "It's rare, but it happens."

As Stephanie made her way down the hall, the distant sound of Alex slamming down the phone reached her ears. Ignoring Linda's advice, her concern spurred her to stick her head into his office. "Is everything all right?"

Alex looked up from his desk, his typically composed demeanor marred by white lines of tension at the corners of his mouth. In response to her question, he growled, "No. The contractor had an entire shipment of damaged materials. It will be a week before he can replace them. We can't start the new job on time because of the re-bar we need for the concrete. That throws us a week behind on final payment."

"Can you tell your clients there will be a delay with starting?" Stephanie inquired, trying to offer a practical solution.

Alex let out a deep sigh, his voice tinged with frustration. "Sure. But that doesn't make a good impression, does it?"

The snap in his voice made Stephanie wince, but she continued, "It's bound to happen now and then."

She waited, wondering if she should have spoken up. Alex ran his fingers through his hair and sighed once more. "I know. I just didn't need it to happen right now."

"Bad things are never convenient," Stephanie observed, hoping her words offered some solace.

He looked at her with his sky-blue eyes that threatened to drown her in their depths. As she waited for his reaction, she resolved to leave the room if he took out his frustration on her again.

She wondered if he sensed her intention, when shaking his head slowly, he said, "I can't excuse negligence. Still, this isn't the contractor's fault. "

"It's all right. I know you're upset," Stephanie replied.

"I have to call the new client to tell him our schedule has changed," Alex explained, taking a deep breath.

"It's possible he won't mind," Stephanie suggested, trying to inject a note of optimism.

Alex scrunched his brows, his expression contemplative. "We'll see."

Deciding to give him some space, Stephanie retreated to her office, hoping that the upcoming call would bring positive news.

Linda had been right. This glitch in the plans had put Alex in a bad mood. Stephanie had been excited to share her research on newspaper and internet advertising to expand the company into southwestern Colorado. However, now wasn't the time to discuss it.

As she worked on the designs for her project, her attention was wholly consumed by the task at hand. The terraced garden held her focus, offering a welcome distraction from the day's earlier tensions.

Later in the afternoon, Alex reappeared with a solemn expression, which told her it wasn't good news. "Thompson insists we meet the cut-off date since he can't reschedule the grand opening," he explained.

Stephanie immediately asked, "What do we do?"

"We meet the deadline. I'll negotiate with the contractor to hire an extra crew. It'll cut into our profits, but it's better than losing the whole job," Alex responded with a weary look, far too early in the day for such exhaustion.

She couldn't help but wonder if Daniel had kept him up the previous night, as small children often did. "Would you like some coffee?" she offered.

A smile that didn't quite reach his eyes graced his lips as he replied, "I'd never ask you to get it for me, but since you're offering, I won't turn it down. Daniel was up twice last night, and the fatigue isn't helping me with my problems."

"You're right. I offered, and I don't mind. I'll be right back with it," Stephanie said, quickly heading to the company lounge.

Pouring steaming coffee from the carafe into a cup, she added two packets of sweetener. Returning to Alex's office, she found him still on the phone. He sounded as if he were in the midst of an intense discussion.

Setting the mug on the corner of his desk, she didn't interrupt and left quietly, mindful of the importance of the conversation.

As she reached the office door, she heard him say, "So, we're agreed to split the cost for the extra crew?"

Pausing for a moment to eavesdrop, she wondered about the contractor's response. She then heard Alex say, "Okay. Have them start the week after next when the new shipment comes."

In her own office, she returned to her design work, focusing on the intricate details of her project.

It was nearly the end of the workday when Alex approached her office again, his face expressing a hint of relief. "The contractor isn't happy with doubling up the crew, but the client will be pleased."

Stephanie studied his expression and inquired, "So it's worked out?"

The lines of tension remained at the corners of his eyes as he responded, "When I explained the situation, he was willing to split the cost."

"That's good it won't all fall back on you," Stephanie said, trying to offer some reassurance.

Alex shook his head, seemingly burdened by the financial implications. "It's still going to be expensive. We may have to put off your idea about expanding for a while."

A pang of disappointment shot through her. She had been so excited to share her plans with him and hoped they could still go forward. However, he owned the business and made the decisions. She was only an employee.

Sitting across from him, Stephanie let her thoughts wander, imagining what it would be like to be partners, collaborating on projects and planning for the future. She quickly shook off these thoughts. They were her fantasies, and Alex was not just her boss, but he was also a father and a widower. The boundaries of their relationship were clear.

"It's all right. My idea can wait until we get past this problem," Stephanie assured him, hoping she sounded understanding.

He offered a small smile, and she wondered if he was also dealing with a sense of disappointment, perhaps the feeling of being overwhelmed by the responsibilities of his business and family.

"Thank you for understanding," he said.

She fought the urge to take the conversation further, to explore the possibilities of their partnership in more detail. Instead, she shifted the focus to work. "Will your guys be done with their job in time to help the contractor and his crew?"

Alex shook his head. "No. I'm sending them out to your project. Since they're not used to working with the other crew, they'd probably get in the way."

"Like too many cooks in a kitchen?" Stephanie asked, offering a light-hearted metaphor.

He nodded with a hint of a smile, the weariness in his eyes still evident. "Exactly."

Rubbing his chin, he shifted the topic of conversation. "We got a call this morning from a residence in the Foothills area. They have an acre and want to put in sprinklers, grass, shrubs, and flowers. You think you could run out and look at it?"

Stephanie responded with eagerness, ready to take on the new project. "Sure! When do you want me to go?"

"I've got their number. You can call and set up an appointment. I want you to know I appreciate your dedication to detail. It's a weight off my shoulders."

Warmth filled Stephanie at the appreciation in his words. "Though I love every part of this job, the details are the most fun."

He managed to smile, though the weariness lingered. "Will you take a raincheck and keep me advised on the Foothills job?"

"Of course," Stephanie agreed, appreciative of the trust he placed in her abilities.

As she prepared to leave, Alex called to her as she locked her office. "When are you moving in with Mandy?"

She turned to see him peering at her from his desk chair. "I'm all packed, and the landlord let me out of my lease. I'm moving in tomorrow night."

Alex surprised her with his offer. "I'll get a sitter for Daniel and help you move."

She knew he cherished the time with his son, and it wasn't a small sacrifice on his part. "Daniel needs to be with you. I can manage fine. There are only boxes since my apartment came completely furnished."

Alex insisted. "I really want to help. You'll still need a hand with the boxes, and it will go faster with the two of us. Besides, my SUV will hold more than your car, so it will take fewer trips, and you won't waste gas."

Stephanie recognized the genuine kindness in his offer. "When you put it that way, I have to accept. I don't want to be uneconomical!"

"What time should I have the sitter come?" Alex inquired.

"I'd like to start carrying things over as early as possible. I figured on buying a burger on the way home and then loading the car."

"How about I meet you at your place at six o'clock?" Alex suggested. "That gives me time to feed Daniel."

"Whenever you can get there is fine. I appreciate the help," Stephanie agreed, grateful for his assistance.

"I owe you for watching him when I went to dinner with our client," Alex added, trying to balance the scale of their relationship.

While she maintained a composed expression, Stephanie felt a twinge of disappointment. She had hoped he enjoyed her company, even if it involved work. Still, she understood that he was trying to maintain a sense of fairness.

With the details settled, Stephanie went home, her thoughts filled with anticipation of her new living arrangements and the gratitude she felt for Alex's generosity.

Mandy called that evening to express her excitement. "I have your room all cleaned and ready. I had fun stocking the hall bathroom with bubble bath and lotion. I want you to have what you need to relax after a long day."

"That's so sweet! Alex is getting a sitter for Daniel to help me move my boxes," Stephanie shared.

Mandy, ever the gracious host, offered another solution. "Oh, nonsense. I'll keep Daniel. That way, he can see his dad while you two bring things here. I'll call Alex and tell him."

Stephanie said, "This is a good solution. He's a precious little boy, and I didn't want to separate them."

Mandy reassured her. "He can have supper with me. I'll make a snack meal for all of us. You and Alex can take a break after your first trip and eat a bite."

The warmth in Mandy's voice touched Stephanie's heart. She already felt welcome and wanted. Her determination to be helpful and good company was strengthened by Mandy's kindness.

As the conversation ended, Stephanie surveyed her apartment, ensuring she hadn't forgotten to pack anything for the move. She opened cupboards and closets to be sure there was nothing of hers that she'd left behind.

Satisfied that everything was in order, Stephanie prepared for the last night she would spend in this bed. Tomorrow, when she got home from work, she would pack her sheets, pillows, and blanket and spend the night in her new bedroom.

IN THE MORNING, SHE dressed and headed to work, looking forward to moving in with

Mandy that evening.

She greeted Linda upon her arrival and shared the news. "I'm moving in tonight with Mandy."

Linda offered a supportive response. "I hear Alex is helping you move, and Mandy is watching Daniel."

"News travels fast around here. He is going to help me," Stephanie confirmed.

Linda 's expression was filled with understanding. "Alex tries to help everybody. Sometimes he spreads himself thin."

Stephanie wondered if she were imposing on his generosity. "I was afraid that was the case when he offered. I'll ask him again if he still has time."

Linda assured her, "He'd never go back on a promise to help."

Stephanie nodded, considering how fortunate she was to have such support. "I know. I feel bad about taking him away from Daniel, even for one evening."

"It's too late this time. It's good to be aware of his generosity," Linda added. "Does Mandy have you going to her church yet?"

"No. She hasn't said anything about it," Stephanie replied.

"Mandy loves that place. I figured she'd invited you," Linda shared.

"No, but I'd like to go. I haven't had time to find a church yet," Stephanie admitted.

"Alex and his late wife attended the same church as Mandy. They had lots of friends there. It helped Alex get through the tragedy," Linda told her.

"It sounds like a church I would like. I'll go next Sunday," Stephanie said, showing her eagerness to become a part of this new community.

Linda's smile was reassuring. "I'm sure you'll find them friendly."

Stephanie thanked Linda and proceeded to her office, her thoughts brimming with anticipation for her upcoming move and her introduction to the new church community.

CHAPTER EIGHT

WHEN STEPHANIE OPENED the door for Alex to help her move the boxes, his gaze was drawn to her wavy, dark locks, which were elegantly clipped back in a barrette. All day his eagerness to assist her in moving to Mandy's house had filled his thoughts. The only times they had spent together outside the office were during her visits to Linda's home for supper and when she briefly babysat Daniel.

Stephanie's face glistened with a slight sheen of moisture, a clear sign of her hard work. Alex wondered where she found her boundless energy. He often felt completely drained by the time he returned home each day, though he understood that her life lacked the demanding tasks of caring for and interacting with a toddler each evening.

"I was slower than I meant to be getting Daniel to Mandy's house," he said by way of apology.

"I understand. I'm grateful you're here."

Glancing around the living room at the stack of boxes, he asked, "Are you ready to start moving these out?"

Stephanie nodded. Gratitude shone in her eyes. "I am, and I appreciate your help. How many boxes will fit in your SUV?"

With a thoughtful gaze, Alex assessed her neatly stacked boxes, each one ready to be carried. "With the seats down, I expect we can move about eight of these at a time."

Stephanie said. "I have twenty boxes in total. I got rid of a lot of things before I came here, and I left some other items at my parents' house. If I take a couple of boxes in my car, we should be able to do it in three trips."

With a quizzical smile, Alex inquired, "Have you marked any of the boxes as fragile?"

Stephanie nodded as she pointed to a box. "My dishes are in this one, though they're quite cheap and not very breakable. I've also got my laptop in its case. That's about the only valuable or fragile items I have in there."

Alex wasn't surprised by Stephanie's practical approach. Unlike his late wife, Kelly, Stephanie appeared to prioritize functionality over extravagance. With Kelly, every trip meant mountains of luggage and double-checking to ensure they hadn't forgotten anything.

He smiled, appreciating Stephanie's no-nonsense nature. As they worked side by side, Alex realized that he longed to know more about her, such as her likes and dislikes. What did she like to read? Did she enjoy action movies?

Together, they sorted the boxes, with Alex handling the heavier ones and Stephanie taking care of the lighter ones. This collaborative effort gave Alex the opportunity to ask more questions. "Did you grow up in the southeast?"

Stephanie paused for a moment after shoving a box into his car and met his gaze. "Yes, I lived in Georgia for most of my life. A couple of years ago, my parents moved to Florida."

Alex continued the conversation, a hint of curiosity in his voice. "What kinds of activities did you engage in while living in Georgia?"

Stephanie's eyes sparkled with memories. "I hiked, played tennis, sang in the school choir, and during the summers, I worked at a theme park. Once I graduated, I went on to college at the University of Georgia."

"It sounds like you kept quite busy," Alex observed.

Stephanie nodded with a smile. "I couldn't stand not having anything to do. My mom used to shuttle me around to various activities when I was in grade school. She believed that keeping me active would keep me out of trouble."

A touch of admiration filled Alex's voice. "It must have worked. I can't imagine you were ever into drugs or heavy drinking."

Stephanie chuckled. "No, I was pretty much a straight arrow. What about you? What kind of activities did you do as a kid?"

As they entered the house with more boxes, Alex began sharing his own experiences. "I was always an outdoorsy kid. My dad had bird dogs, and we spent a lot of time with them. I played baseball and basketball at school, was on the debate team, and I watched a lot of movies."

Curiosity got the best of Stephanie. "What kind of movies do you like? Did you go to the cinema with pretty dates?"

'I've always liked action movies and I usually went with my buddies, who weren't so pretty."

Stephanie giggled and said, "I like action movies, but I also enjoy comedies. I'm not a fan of sad ones; they tend to stay with me after they're over, making me feel depressed."

Alex concurred with a knowing nod. "I feel the same way. Life already throws enough challenges our way without seeking out more in movies."

They closed their cars, ready to head back to Mandy's house with the first load of boxes. When they arrived, the scene that greeted them was heartwarming. Daniel was sitting at the table, happily spooning macaroni and cheese into his mouth.

Mandy welcomed them with warm hospitality. "I hope you don't mind that we started without you. The little guy was hungry."

Alex's gaze roamed over the spread of cold cuts, rolls, dill pickles, sliced tomatoes, chips, and a bowl of homemade macaroni and cheese. The delightful aromas of dill and assorted meats stirred his appetite. "You went through a lot of trouble here, but it looks absolutely delicious."

Mandy beamed at them. "I figured that box movers get hungry. I hope you both enjoy my little supper."

She handed them Rosewood china plates, and Alex's lips curved into a grateful smile. "We appreciate your hospitality!"

As they filled their plates, Daniel held a pickle slice in his small hand as he grinned at his dad. "Yummy."

With an affectionate pat on Daniel's head, Alex chuckled. "You like pickles, huh?"

Glancing at Daniel's nearly empty plastic bowl, Alex said, "You've nearly finished all your macaroni and cheese, too. You must have been pretty hungry."

Daniel took a drink from his Sippy cup, "Mik."

"Milk, yes. You have milk," Alex confirmed, grinning at his son.

Mandy poured glasses of iced tea for their refreshment, and they sat down to satisfy their appetites before resuming the moving process.

Stephanie turned her attention to the practical details. "I have four boxes of dishes and kitchen articles. Where should I store them?"

With a thoughtful expression, Mandy pondered the options. "If they're not too heavy, we can put them in the attic. I don't keep anything else up there except for holiday decorations."

Concerned about logistics, Stephanie inquired, "Do you have stairs to the attic?"

Mandy, with a nod, replied, "There's a pull-down staircase in the garage."

"Great," Alex said. "I'll plan to place those boxes in the garage for now and carry them up later, after we get everything here."

Stephanie's gratitude was evident in her smile. "I appreciate all the help you're providing."

With a casual gesture at his plate, Alex emphasized, "I'm being well compensated."

The three shared a warm conversation, basking in the convivial atmosphere of the moment. Meanwhile, Daniel finished his meal, and, with the promise of more fun, playfully slid out of his chair. "Hole me!"

Eager to embrace his son, Alex picked him up, smiling broadly. "I love holding you. You're such a snuggle bug."

The three of them nibbled on cookies and shared some sweet memories before it was time to make a second trip for more boxes.

With reluctance, Alex returned Daniel to his chair, placing a tender kiss on his son's head. "I have to make another trip for more boxes. You stay with Grandma Mandy, and I'll be back soon."

The prospect of his dad leaving again didn't sit well with Daniel, and he appeared on the verge of complaint. Mandy, however, came to the rescue. "Why don't we head to the backyard to see if we can spot the moon?"

"Moon?" Daniel's interest was piqued.

"Yes, come along." Mandy extended her hand, and Daniel eagerly accepted it. She guided him away from the table, leading him toward the backyard.

As Alex watched this scene unfold, he noticed Stephanie watching them with a tender expression. He appreciated the soft side he saw in this industrious woman. It left him with a warm feeling deep inside.

With practicality at the forefront of her mind, Stephanie suggested, "Let's put away the cold cuts. It'll only take a minute."

"Sure," Alex agreed.

Working efficiently and together, they concluded the task, preparing to head back to Stephanie's apartment for another load of boxes. In the midst of this collaboration, Alex felt the need to ask Stephanie, "You like kids, don't you?"

Stephanie paused for a moment, surprised by the unexpected question. "I do. Why do you ask?"

"It's the way you look at Daniel," Alex explained, his gaze revealing his keen observation.

Stephanie offered a warm smile. "He's such a cute kid!"

Alex continued to share his thoughts. "I agree. However, he takes after his mother. She had light brown hair and a face shaped like his."

Intrigued, Stephanie inquired further, her curiosity getting the best of her. "She must have been very pretty."

With a hint of melancholy in his voice, Alex retrieved a beige billfold from his pocket and flipped it open to reveal a picture of a young woman with radiant dark eyes. Stephanie's gaze lingered on the lovely face that had been Daniel's mother.

As he held the billfold, Alex felt the ever-present ache of loss. Kelly's absence was a heavy weight on his heart, an emptiness that refused to be filled. His mind often played tricks on him, making him imagine that she was still there, pouring coffee in the morning or smiling at him when he returned home. The pain of her absence continued to affect him, leaving him wondering if time would ever truly heal his wounds.

"She was beautiful," Stephanie whispered with a touch of empathy. "It must be comforting to have a little boy who reminds you of her."

With a quiver in his voice, Alex shared his emotional journey. "When I first lost her, having Daniel gave me the incentive to get myself back together. I don't know what I would have done without him."

Stephanie understood the depth of his connection with his son. "I can see how he provides you with comfort and a sense of purpose."

As Alex put away the billfold, he contemplated the complexities of his feelings. He realized that he was enjoying Stephanie's company. Was that disloyal to Kelly?

Kelly and Stephanie would have liked each other. The similarities were undeniable. Stephanie exuded an infectious energy and optimism, much like Kelly. Their shared traits of determination and single-mindedness painted a vivid picture of two kindred spirits.

He must maintain boundaries in his relationship with Stephanie, he thought. He must remember to keep it strictly professional. One evening of camaraderie wouldn't hurt, but he knew that Stephanie was not a permanent fixture in his life. Perhaps, one day, she might outgrow her role. She might leave his company to open her own business. If that day came, he didn't want her to take his heart with her.

Together, they loaded the next set of boxes and transported them to Mandy's house. Inside, they found Daniel sprawled on the floral sofa, absorbed in a children's program about counting puppies. He was blissfully unaware of his dad's absence as went for the last load of boxes.

Returning to Mandy's home with the final load of boxes, the promise of fresh iced tea was a welcome respite. Alex eagerly sipped his glass, driven by his fatigue and the looming task of getting Daniel ready for bed.

Children's bedtime rituals were a challenge, with the little boy sometimes crying about changing clothes and brushing teeth. Alex's weariness occasionally overtook him, and he would retire when Daniel went to bed.

Stephanie and Alex placed boxes of clothing and personal items into her bedroom, leaving only a handful of boxes for the attic.

Mandy intervened, urging them to stop, saying, "You've done enough for tonight. These can stay in the living room until someone has time to carry them up. If I bake Jason a plate of scones, he might do it."

Alex, intrigued by the mention of scones, raised an eyebrow as he asked, "You mean I could have scones if I come back?"

Mandy confirmed with a warm smile, "Of course."

With a playful grin, Alex teased. "Hold onto those scones for me!"

Mandy playfully added, "I'll do that. I bet little Daniel would like one, too."

Alex readily agreed, saying, "You have a deal."

As the evening concluded, Alex scooped up his drowsy son from the couch. "You're tired, aren't you, buddy? Let's get you home to bed."

Turning to Mandy, he thanked her for her hospitality. "Supper was great."

Mandy reciprocated with a warm smile. "My pleasure. I love having company."

Stephanie expressed her gratitude as well, acknowledging the heartwarming assistance. "It was nice of both of you to help me."

While he tried to suppress the warmth in his heart upon hearing her thanks, Alex reflected on the evening. Tonight, he'd enjoyed the company of a smart and attractive woman, which was a stark contrast to his solitary existence dominated by work and caring for Daniel for almost two years. Tonight's brief companionship was a welcome change of pace, and he couldn't deny the enjoyment.

On the journey back home, he hummed softly, lost in his thoughts. After tending to his son and putting him to bed, he lay in the stillness of the night, pondering the prospect of ending his self-imposed isolation. It had been nearly two years since Kelly's passing, and the idea of dating resurfaced for the first time. Though he knew it couldn't be Stephanie due to their professional relationship, he began considering other avenues to meet new people and, perhaps, to find companionship.

ON SATURDAY MORNING, Mandy watched Daniel while Alex carried the boxes to the attic. Upon finishing the task, Alex was welcomed by the inviting aroma of hot blueberry scones.

Curiosity piqued, Alex inquired about Stephanie's whereabouts.

Mandy replied, "She went shopping for winter clothes to get them on off-season sale. The things she brought are fine for summer and fall but not the coldest part of winter."

Despite his attempts to suppress any disappointment that Stephanie wasn't present, Alex conceded that it was only because he had spent the entire week working closely with her. Resolving to move forward, he mulled over the idea of attending church tomorrow. There, he would have a chance to enrich his spiritual life, meet new people, reconnect with old friends, and distract himself from his growing thoughts about Stephanie.

As everyone savored the treats, Alex asked Mandy, "How are things working out with both of you?"

Mandy added a dollop of whipped cream to her scone and said, "She's a terrific girl. I love having someone to talk to in the evening."

Alex was eager to learn more about Stephanie's background. "I guess you're getting to know each other well."

Mandy happily shared an intriguing fact about Stephanie's past. "Yes. She's very interesting. Did you know she worked for the Forest Service for a couple of summers when she was in college? She knows all about trees and wildlife. One time she was walking near a stream and took pictures of some black bears fishing."

Intrigued, Alex said, "I'd like to see those. Where did she work?"

"In the Chattahoochee-Oconee National Forest. It's a beautiful place. The plants and trees inspired her to pursue a landscaping career."

"That sounds like an awesome experience. I'm grateful it led to her coming to work for me here."

He glanced at Daniel and saw that he was covered in crumbs and had whipped cream smeared across his face. "You're a mess, mister. I need to wipe you off. Then, you and I will make a trip to the grocery store. After that, we might make it to Berg Park and feed the ducks."

Daniel, thrilled at the prospect, repeated, "Ducks?"

"Yes. You like them, don't you?"

Daniel nodded eagerly, ready to leave the table.

Alex cautioned his son. "We have to go shopping first. Be a good boy while we're at the store, okay?"

Daniel nodded in agreement.

Mandy told Alex, "I'll tell Stephanie you moved the boxes for her."

Alex added playfully, "We even saved her a couple of scones."

Mandy joined in the playful banter, chuckling. "We're generous, aren't we?"

Alex lifted Daniel onto his shoulders, and the joyful child laughed as they left the house. They set off to complete their tasks, replenishing groceries and indulging in a leisurely visit to Berg Park to feed the ducks.

At the park, the ducks waddled toward them, and Daniel was enthralled. His little hand grasped a fistful of corn, which he eagerly tossed to the waiting waterfowl. The vivid green heads of the Mallards glistened in the sunlight as they enjoyed the impromptu feast.

Soon, they had fed the last of the corn to the ducks, and the birds gradually dispersed, heading back to the water. However, Daniel was determined to have them stay. Frowning, he implored, "Back!"

Understanding his son's reluctance to leave, Alex gently explained, "We can't make them stay here. They want to swim."

Despite Alex's best efforts, Daniel persisted. "Back," he insisted, his eyes filling with tears.

The signs of an impending meltdown were apparent. Alex knew they needed to head home for Daniel to take a nap.

Reassuringly, he said, "It's home for us now. We'll come back again soon."

As he expected, Daniel fell asleep on the way home. Alex carried him inside to his room, lovingly decorated by Kelly with train wallpaper, his name on a plaque, and a smiling train clock on the wall.

The rocker sat by the window where Kelly had rocked her newborn. Sudden tears blurred his eyes at the memory. He had to get on with his life. Attending church tomorrow would be a new beginning. The thought made him nervous, yet he was determined to carry through.

CHAPTER NINE

STEPHANIE DID HER BEST to quell her anxiety about attending a new church. She took Mandy's word that everyone would be friendly, but the idea of mingling with so many strangers still made her palms feel clammy.

While she carefully applied mascara and brushed her hair into soft waves, she noticed the fine lines forming at the corners of her eyes. She reminded herself that aging was a natural process that she shouldn't dwell on.

When she joined Mandy in the kitchen, Mandy was finishing her coffee. She greeted Stephanie with a compliment. "You look nice. Are you ready?"

Taking a deep breath, Stephanie admitted, "Yes, but I'm a little nervous. Meeting large groups of new people has never been my strong suit."

Understanding Stephanie's apprehension, Mandy offered some reassuring words. "I get it. It can be overwhelming at first, but I promise, after a few visits, you'll feel right at home."

With a grateful smile, Stephanie replied, "I know, I always do."

Together, they headed to Mandy's car. Stephanie took her place in the passenger seat and shivered slightly in the cool morning air.

As they made their way to the red brick church, Stephanie admired the newly forming leaves on the trees, their branches no longer stark as they reached for the vibrant blue sky. She was struck by the beauty of God's creation, a sentiment deepened by her previous experience working with the Forest Service.

Upon arriving at the church, they joined the other worshippers as they made their way inside. Mandy introduced her to friends and acquaintances while Stephanie tried not to feel overwhelmed by the new faces. She silently hoped no one would be offended if she couldn't remember all their names.

As they entered the sanctuary, the dark polished wooden pews created an atmosphere of formality. Stained glass windows depicting the life of Christ gazed down on them.

Mandy's face lit up when she spotted Lissa and Jason, and Stephanie followed her to the pew. The pianist played softly as the choir members filed in, and soon, Alex entered and took a seat at the end of their pew, not noticing them,

Mandy whispered to Stephanie, "He's committed to being a regular attendee again. It's been difficult for him since Kelly passed."

Stephanie couldn't help but wonder if she was part of the reason Alex had decided to attend church today. Had he known she would be here? The idea made her feel less like a stranger, and she began to relax as they joined the congregation in singing a song that celebrated God's grace and majesty.

The pastor's message seemed tailor-made for Alex's grief. Stephanie was moved by the sermon's emphasis on finding solace in God's presence and the promise of reuniting with loved ones in Heaven and eliminating the pain of separation.

Curious about Alex's response, she tried to steal glances to read his expression. Had the sermon offered him the comfort he needed? Though he had been separated early in life from Kelly, the pastor's words were a reminder that he would see her again one day.

When the service concluded and the announcements were made, Stephanie watched as Alex left through the opposite side of the church, unaware that Mandy and Stephanie had been sitting in the same pew.

Nonetheless, she had enjoyed seeing him and had hoped for a chance to speak with him. As they left the church with Lissa and Jason, Lissa asked, "Did you like the service?"

Admiring Lissa, a dark-haired pixie with sea-green eyes, Stephanie assured her, "I loved the service. It reminds me of my church back in Georgia. We always sang a few older hymns during each service, as well."

Mandy said, "I'm happy you enjoyed it. Would you like to stay for Sunday School?"

Stephanie's stomach clenched. Joining a new group of people made her nervous. She preferred to know a few of them first. Still, she didn't want to keep Mandy from attending her class. She hesitated before replying. "Sure. Lead the way."

As she walked with Lissa and Jason, Stephanie took in her surroundings. "This is quite a long hallway."

Lissa's response was heartwarming. "Full of the most beautiful people I've ever known. They've been good to us."

Jason chimed in with a chuckle, "They plotted to get us together."

"It looks like they succeeded," Stephanie said with a smile.

Lissa added, "It was mostly Grandma Mandy."

Jason agreed. "She's quite the matchmaker. Watch out!"

Examining the happy couple, Stephanie remarked, "I don't think she did badly with you two. Maybe I'll hire her!"

Their laughter filled the corridor as they agreed that Mandy would do an excellent job, and it would even be free. Stephanie genuinely meant that she would appreciate Mandy's assistance in finding the right person to share her life with. She had prayed about it and yearned for a love that would stand the test of time, much like the love her parents shared.

Lissa and Jason led her to the singles class where Stephanie glanced at her surroundings. Posters of scripture, prints of Jesus healing the blind man, and depicting the Last Supper covered the walls. What caught her attention, however, was Alex standing beside one of the posters.

Their eyes met, and Stephanie felt as if they were the only two people in the room. Her anticipation grew, trying to interpret his expression.

Instead of a smile, he broke eye contact, leaving Stephanie feeling lonely and confused, adrift in a sea of voices. Why didn't he smile when he saw her?

Before she could retreat, one of the class members spotted the trio at the door and said, "Hi! Do we have a visitor?"

A blond woman with light blue eyes, who appeared to be in her early thirties, took Stephanie by the elbow. "Come in and join us."

While Lissa chuckled, Stephanie decided she couldn't make a quick exit now. Melanie guided her into the classroom. After being greeted by several other members, Stephanie took a seat. Moments later, Alex sat down next to her.

Her heart leapt. Instead of ignoring her, he smiled and said, "I didn't know you were visiting today."

"Mandy talked me into it," Stephanie replied. "What brought you here?"

"I haven't been to church in a while," Alex explained. "I've missed the people. Daniel needs it, too."

Stephanie said, "It's interesting that we both decided to come on the same day."

Before he could answer, the class began with the teacher opening with a prayer. When the teacher began the lesson, Alex tried to focus on his words. However, with Stephanie sitting beside him, he was constantly aware of her presence. The gentle scent of lavender from her shampoo was soothing, and her presence was distracting.

They talked about examining the idols in their lives, and Stephanie pondered her own actions. "I want my way a lot," she whispered, "but sometimes God prospers me. Other times he gives me trials and discipline, much like a father does with his children."

Alex could see the wisdom in her words and shared his thoughts. "He doesn't always grant my every wish, either."

Stephanie was pleased to see that Alex was opening up about his spiritual journey. It gave her a sense of connection. As the class concluded and people started to leave, Stephanie walked with Alex into the corridor. "What did you think of the rest of the lesson?" she asked.

He admitted, "I felt convicted to overhaul my priorities. I'm guilty of having a few idols."

Stephanie nodded in agreement, sharing her own feelings. "So am I. I sometimes forget that trials and chastisement are His way of making us grow. It's just like a father disciplining his child."

Her words resonated with Alex, who had been struggling with resentment after Kelly's death. "He doesn't give in to my every wish, either," he said.

At the nursery, Alex stood in line to pick up Daniel. When he had his son in his arms, he nuzzled the child's cheek. "Did you have fun?"

Daniel's excitement couldn't be contained as he enthusiastically mentioned toys. "Toys fun," he said, before pointing to his mouth. "Crackers."

With a warm smile, Alex responded, "You got a snack, didn't you?"

As they walked through the foyer, Daniel began to shout, "Grandma," and waved his hand. Alex had to gently explain that his grandma wasn't there, but it was actually Grandma Mandy. Daniel was eager to see her, and his eyes lit up at the sight of Stephanie. "Play?"

Although Alex reminded Daniel that it was time for lunch, the child wasn't hungry yet.

Mandy suggested that they have lunch together at her house with a little playtime for Daniel.

On the ride home with Mandy, Stephanie tried to suppress her eagerness to see Alex again at lunch. She knew she had to put a stop to any burgeoning feelings, as it was clear he was still mourning his late wife. She doubted he would reciprocate her affections. Nevertheless, every time they locked eyes, she thought she saw a glimmer of longing in his gaze.

During the drive home, Mandy commented on how cute Daniel was and brought up the idea that he needed a mother's touch. Stephanie agreed that Alex needed to find someone who would love Daniel like her own child. Stephanie could not admit that she had fantasized about raising Daniel with Alex.

As they arrived home, Stephanie reflected on the futility of her attraction to her boss. She needed to remain focused on her professional relationship with him. While Mandy's hints were well-intentioned, Mandy didn't know the whole story. The path to romance with Alex was laden with obstacles she doubted she could overcome.

CHAPTER TEN

WHEN MANDY REMINDED Daniel that she would rock him to sleep after lunch, it elicited a hopeful request from the toddler. With arms outstretched, Daniel looked up at Stephanie. "Book?"

Stephanie met Daniel's gaze and replied, "Did you bring a book?"

Alex, standing nearby, reached into Daniel's bag, and handed Stephanie a stack of well-loved children's books. "He always has several in here."

As Mandy began setting out lunch, Daniel nestled into Stephanie's lap. Together, they delved into an ABC book, its pages filled with captivating, rhyming illustrations. Daniel eagerly pointed at each picture, naming them before turning the page.

Stephanie admired the child's attention span. "He focuses well for a child who's barely two."

"Being read to has always been a favorite activity," Alex remarked. "I'm lucky if I can get him to sleep with only three stories."

Grinning, Stephanie shared her own love for books. "I love reading, too. As a kid, I haunted the public library. I checked out five or six books each week and read them."

Curious about her tastes, Alex asked, "What sort of stories did you like?"

Thinking back to her childhood, Stephanie recalled, "I usually picked mystery and adventure. How about you?"

Alex's taste in books took a different direction. "I wasn't much of a fiction reader. I liked how-to books and technical reading."

Stephanie chuckled, appreciating their differences. "It sounds like you were one smart kid."

With a self-deprecating laugh, Alex replied, "No, just not very imaginative. I like reading things that teach me how to do something."

Stephanie tilted her head, her eyes studying him. "I'm afraid that would put me to sleep."

His response was accompanied by a playful grin. "Sometimes, it put me to sleep, as well."

As Mandy set the cold cuts on the table, she interjected, "Lunch is ready. Better dig in."

The small group gathered around the table. Mandy turned to Alex and requested, "Would you say a prayer?"

Without hesitation, Alex agreed. "Of course." The room quieted as they bowed their heads, and Alex began to speak. "Lord, we thank You for this food and the opportunity to share it. Help us to love You more each day. Amen."

Though the prayer was simple, it carried a heartfelt sincerity that brought sudden tears to Stephanie's eyes. She found herself admiring Alex's strong faith, knowing he loved his son and was a good father, despite the pain of losing Kelly.

Her growing attraction to him was undeniable, intensified by his appearance. In his powder-blue cotton shirt and neatly trimmed dark hair, his striking looks only deepened her feelings. Yet, she was also aware of the inherent complications in pursuing anything more with him.

Mandy noticed Stephanie's contemplative expression when Alex finished the prayer. "You look thoughtful, dear. Is everything all right?"

Shaking off her inner turmoil, Stephanie replied, "I'm fine, just a little tired from the morning. I enjoyed it, though."

"I loved having your company on the way to church. I usually make the drive alone," Mandy said.

"I don't know if I would have had the courage to go alone. Facing crowds of strangers isn't my strong suit," Stephanie admitted.

Alex interjected, trying to offer reassurance. "You do fine dealing with clients at work."

Stephanie nodded. "That's one-on-one. Large groups are different. I feel awkward in them."

Her cheeks grew warm under Alex's penetrating gaze. The two shared a moment of silent understanding.

Alex then commented, "You're an intricate woman, Stephanie. Did you grow up in a small town? Maybe you just got used to knowing everyone."

Stephanie considered his question, recalling her background. "I've lived and worked in Savannah. It's pretty big, so I don't think that's it."

Alex responded with understanding. "We all have issues with something."

Curious about his own concerns, Stephanie contemplated asking about them, but it felt premature to delve into such personal matters without him volunteering the information.

Daniel began to squirm in his chair, signaling the end of his lunch. "I done."

Alex informed his son, "You'll have to stay in here with us."

"I'm finished. I can take him into the living room and read a story if that's okay," Mandy offered.

Stephanie's heart raced at the thought of being alone with Alex outside of work. However, her growing attraction was becoming a source of inner turmoil when they were in close quarters together.

Hoping to shift the conversation to a less personal topic, Stephanie asked Alex, "What does our work schedule look like tomorrow?"

Alex shared their plans. "We have three client meetings, and both of us will have to check on jobs. Then, I have a new customer looking at plans. I'd like you to sit in to offer advice."

Grateful for his invitation, Stephanie tried to contain her enthusiasm. "I'd be happy to contribute!"

Alex knitted his brows, offering her constructive feedback. "I think sometimes you hold back a little. You won't offend me if you critique my plans. I'm always looking for ways to improve them."

His words took Stephanie by surprise. "My previous employer was a wonderful man and taught me a lot. However, he wouldn't have appreciated having me suggest changes to his plans. If you feel differently, I'll speak up."

Alex responded with unwavering support. "Good. We'll build a stronger client base by combining the best both of us can offer. I may not always take advice, but I promise to welcome it."

Her admiration for him deepened as she nodded. In her experience, humility was a rare trait among those with creative talent. The open and supportive atmosphere he fostered was refreshing.

He continued to study her with openness in his clear blue eyes, making her heart swell. Despite her efforts to suppress it, her feelings for him had developed into something deeper than professional admiration.

Alex was the most amiable man she had ever met, and his classic good looks only added to her growing attraction. The inner turmoil she felt was inescapable as her thoughts frequently strayed to him even when she wasn't at work. She wondered if he thought about her, too, but she chastised herself for dwelling on the idea.

As they chatted, their conversation meandered to her charming Southern accent, which Alex found appealing. She had worried that it would make her stand out, but he assured her it could be a good thing by making her memorable. The compliment from him warmed her heart, and she responded with a bashful, "Thank you."

However, she wondered whether or not she was reading too much into his words, unsure if he meant anything beyond the simple compliment.

As the conversation continued, they shared more about their experiences and growing up in different places. Alex's parents were still living on the east coast, missing him and Daniel dreadfully. They longed for a visit, and he considered arranging one in the coming months.

Before ending their conversation, they talked about Daniel's growing vocabulary, and Alex's love for his son shone through. He emphasized his appreciation for fatherhood and highlighted the importance of considering his son in all of his life choices.

Later, as Alex drove back home, his thoughts were consumed by Stephanie. Her auburn, curly hair framing her face, her luminous brown eyes, and the softness she exhibited when saying goodbye to Daniel had touched him deeply. He was accustomed to her professional demeanor, but this softer side was genuinely endearing.

Daniel sang softly in his car seat as Alex pondered what he could accomplish while his son napped. Household chores awaited him, from emptying the dishwasher to taking out the trash. He needed to check his email and maybe call his parents. If time permitted, he looked forward to indulging in a chapter or two about planetary weather in the solar system.

Upon arriving home, he carried his sleeping son into the house. As he laid him in bed, he admired Daniel's cherubic face and soft silky hair.

Kelly's memory washed over him as guilt suddenly seized him. He'd enjoyed Stephanie's company, and even though his intentions weren't romantic, he realized he had unconsciously pictured them as a family. This realization frightened him. He hadn't anticipated being attracted to anyone after Kelly's passing.

Conflicted, Alex recognized the need for advice. He thought about speaking with Linda to gain clarity on his emotions before they became too overwhelming. He needed to determine whether or not pursuing a romantic relationship was a realistic possibility.

After he completed his chores, he made a call to his parents. They were eager to see him and Daniel. He knew their hearts ached for a visit. Sadness weighed on him as he considered how long it had been since they'd visited. While he wanted to make them happy, he couldn't guarantee any time off, as an urgent project always seemed to arise at inopportune moments.

Nonetheless, he vowed to work out a visit for Mother's Day and hopefully arrange a flight again during the slower season after summer. When he mentioned this, his parents were overjoyed by the prospect.

As the day wore on, Alex found solace in sitting down with his book. However, when he fell asleep after the second chapter, his mind became a battleground of emotions.

He dreamed of Kelly and Stephanie working together at the firm as tension grew between them. He tried to explain to Kelly that she was the one he loved, but she remained distant. In his dream, he struggled with the complexities of his emotions, feeling disloyal to Kelly and uncertain about his feelings for Stephanie.

When he awoke with a start, Daniel's cries drew him back to reality. His son had awoken from his nap, seeking comfort. As he lifted Daniel into his arms, Alex knew one thing for certain. Whatever choices he made in the future, he would always consider his son's well-being first.

CHAPTER ELEVEN

THE NEXT MORNING, AS Stephanie prepared for work, her thoughts centered on her growing attraction to Alex. She wondered whether he had picked up on her feelings, despite her best efforts to conceal them. Small gestures and comments might have inadvertently revealed her emotions.

She stared at her reflection in the mirror, a furrow forming on her brow. Had she let her feelings escape her tight control, and was Alex aware of the effect he had on her?

Her cheeks flushed with heat, and she couldn't shake the anxiety that perhaps he wished she could rein in her feelings. Having a crush on the boss could potentially create unease for Alex and Linda.

An even worse thought crossed her mind. What if she ended up being pitied for harboring affection for a man whose heart was forever bound to his late wife? The pain of his loss was evident. No matter what her heart was telling her, Stephanie felt a moral obligation to ensure that her feelings were strictly professional.

When Stephanie arrived at the office, Linda was just opening the door. A warm smile spread across her face as she asked, "Did you have a nice weekend?"

Stephanie nodded, her voice filled with enthusiasm. "I did. I love living with Mandy. We cooked dinner together on Saturday night, and I've learned so much about cooking from her."

Linda's eyes sparkled with curiosity. "Have you tried her green chili chicken? It's unbelievable!"

"We haven't had that yet, but I'll make sure to get all the ingredients for her," Stephanie replied.

Linda grinned, teasingly, "Bring me some!"

As they entered the office, Linda asked, "Do you have a busy day ahead?"

Stephanie replied, "I have client meetings and then a job to check on."

Linda playfully retorted, "I remember putting those two things on my calendar to remind you, even though you never forget anything."

Stephanie laughed. "Trust me, I do!"

Alex strolled into the office, his presence commanding attention. He mentioned the morning struggles of getting Daniel settled at the sitter's, and the image of his little boy forgetting his beloved blanket tugged at Stephanie's heartstrings. With a touch of empathy, she remarked, "Poor little guy. His blanket is like a piece of home he carries with him."

"He didn't bring it to Mandy's house for lunch yesterday, and he didn't seem to miss it," Alex said.

Linda, now intrigued, raised an eyebrow. "You were at Mandy's place yesterday?"

"She invited us to lunch after church," Alex explained.

Linda, keenly observant, gave Stephanie a suspicious look that Alex failed to notice, as he nonchalantly stated, "She's such a sweet lady. She's kind to me and Daniel."

Pursing her lips, Linda said, "That's nice of her to include the two of you."

Throughout the morning, Stephanie couldn't shake the feeling of disturbance in Linda's demeanor. If only she knew Linda better, she might inquire about her concerns.

During lunchtime, Linda sought her out, offering, "I just got the mail. Alex has already left for lunch, so I thought I'd bring it to you to see what you want to open and what we should save for him."

Stephanie glanced at the mail and responded, "I can take care of this. None of it looks personal."

Linda seemed to hesitate before finally saying, "It may not be my business, but I wondered if you two are becoming more than business associates? You seem to be spending time outside of work together."

Stephanie struggled to maintain a neutral expression. "He was only there yesterday because Mandy invited him. We're not romantically involved, if that's what you mean."

Linda sounded somewhat disapproving as she said, "That's probably for the best. He'd feel guilty if he dated you. He's not over Kelly, you know."

"Yes, I do know," Stephanie replied, her heart feeling the weight of the truth. Linda's words raised guilty feelings, even though she hadn't done anything wrong.

Linda seemed relieved, saying, "That's good. Are you working through lunch?"

Stephanie nodded. "I brought a sandwich and an apple. I'll probably take a walk when I finish the draft. It looks sunny outside."

Linda added, "You might want to wear your jacket. It was still cool when I went to make a bank deposit."

"Thanks. I'll remember," Stephanie replied.

She stared at the doorway after Linda left, ruminating on how easy it was for people to jump to conclusions. She would need to be more cautious about the signals she was sending.

Re-centering her thoughts on her work, Stephanie reached a stopping point before donning her sweater and heading out. Her wanderings took her to the neighborhood park, a pleasant oasis beyond the confines of the office.

Houses nestled around the outside of the park looked cozy, smoke curling from chimneys, a testament to their snug warmth. Stephanie dreamed of, one day, having her own home, perhaps with a nursery bathed in sunlight, with a sweet baby in a crib, fast asleep. The image of little Daniel flitted across her mind's eye, his round cheeks reminiscent of infancy. It was almost too easy to imagine him as her own.

Stephanie caught herself and reined in her thoughts. Why was she daydreaming about this child when her focus should be on her future family?

She banished the idea of motherhood for the moment and concentrated on the peaceful beauty around her. The cloudless sky painted a serene backdrop for her walk, and a kite stuck high in the branches of a tall elm was a whimsical nod to the March breeze.

The park offered a collection of benches that encircled a grassy central area, an ideal spot for picnics. A pavilion stood at the edge, ready to provide shelter should the weather take a turn.

With a determination to revitalize her exercise routine, Stephanie set a goal to make walking and jogging a regular habit. It was essential, given that her work with Mandy didn't demand much physical exertion. Yard chores were taken care of by Jason, who had already prepared the yard for spring.

She thought of the patch of soil she once tended, where her mother allowed her to plant seeds. Watching those tiny seeds sprout and grow was a marvel that served as a yearly reminder of the distinction between human effort and divine providence.

Stephanie was drawn from her thoughts by the sound of her name. Glancing down the trail, she saw Alex approaching.

"Linda told me you went for a walk. I thought you might have come here. Do you jog, also?"

Her heart raced as she stopped. "I combine walking and jogging. This park is perfect, and the weather is fantastic for outdoor exercise."

Alex nodded and said, "I used to be a runner back in high school. It's been over a year since I've done more than take a walk around the block."

Stephanie responded with understanding. "It's hard with little Daniel."

Alex agreed, saying, "He takes up most of my time. When I get home at night, I want to spend time with him, and I still have to get him fed and ready for bed."

Before thinking it through, Stephanie said, "You look like you're in good shape. Your physique doesn't suggest you've let your fitness slip. Maybe lugging around your little boy keeps you exercised."

Hoping to distract him from her comment about his handsome build, she hurried on to add, "I have time to work out on evenings and weekends, but I don't have a regular exercise program. I often wish I had a dog to motivate me for a daily walk. I think I'd enjoy that."

Alex had a playful suggestion. "Why don't you get a dog?"

With a shake of her head, Stephanie replied, "I'd never impose on Mandy."

Alex offered himself as an alternative, a subtle note of hope in his voice. "I might be able to take the place of a dog. I could encourage you to come here and walk or jog with me every day. It's a great spot for a breather from the office."

Stephanie smiled, even though she realized she should be cautious. "That might work to hold each other accountable. I do plan to spend part of my lunch hour here on days when the weather is nice."

A contemplative look in his eyes, Alex ventured, "I'd like to bring Daniel here for lunch sometimes. He'd love that. We could all have lunch and then he could play and stay out of your way when you jog."

Hope blossomed in Stephanie's heart, as part of her yearned for their meetings not to be solely about Daniel. She chastised herself for even entertaining such thoughts, saying, "Sure, I think that's a wonderful idea! He wouldn't be in my way, and I'd love to see him again."

She couldn't stop herself from agreeing, even though she wondered what others would think, especially Linda. However, at that moment, it didn't matter. Alex had been kind to her, and she genuinely wanted to return that kindness.

"In that case, maybe I'll bring him tomorrow," Alex proposed.

With a glance at his watch, he said, "I need to get back. Take your time and finish your walk. I'll see you when you're done."

Stephanie responded, "My time's up, and I'm ready to go."

AS THEY WALKED TO THE building together, the gentle breeze tugged at Alex's jacket and playfully rustled Stephanie's hair. An urge to brush the silky strands away from her soft, velvety- cheeks welled up in him, but he knew he needed to maintain his professionalism. He had to be careful when he was around her, to keep from falling under the spell of her captivating dark eyes.

The lobby, encased in glass walls, was bathed in sunlight, creating a cheerful atmosphere. They entered and their laughter echoed in the room as Stephanie recounted her lively experience tasting fiery local salsa.

Once they parted at their respective offices, Alex delved into his work, focusing on his clients and the tasks at hand. He told himself that he would see Stephanie again soon and that his eagerness was all about her valuable contributions to the business. However, as he considered the idea of making her a partner, a disquieting feeling arose within him. Could he ever share his enterprise?

He was reminded of the concept of idols from the Bible, and he questioned whether his business had become one. He had justified his dedication to building a secure future for Daniel, but it struck him that perhaps he hadn't made room for anything or anyone else.

When the Fosters arrived for their one o'clock appointment, Stephanie joined them, and Alex was struck again by her poise and beauty. He reminded himself to focus on the clients' needs as he engaged in a discussion about landscaping plans.

After careful consideration, they decided on a patio in the backyard, encircled by a swath of vibrant grass and adorned with Rose of Sharon and Butterfly Bushes.

Lydia Foster was thrilled, exclaiming, "I can't wait for this to get underway! We'll have a beautiful yard just in time for summer."

Stephanie joined in with equal enthusiasm, saying, "Yes, you will!"

Once the clients left, Alex lauded Stephanie for her impeccable designs, admiring her unwavering dedication to her work.

Their eyes met, and Stephanie's gaze sparkled as she said, "I love making people happy, and I'm blessed to be able to do what I enjoy."

The sentiment was reciprocated, and Alex noted, "Your enthusiasm for the job is contagious. The clients sense it."

They momentarily found themselves in an intimate bubble, their connection palpable before they quickly refocused on their professional roles.

Back in his office, Alex had to push Stephanie yet again from his thoughts as he tackled the job of ordering supplies. As the day drew to a close, she popped into his office to provide a quick update on her projects.

"The ground was uneven where the Johnsons want their patio, so it's taking an extra day to prepare. But on the bright side, the Baker job is ahead of schedule. So I guess it all balances out in the end."

Alex acknowledged, "It's par for the course in our trade."

Stephanie nodded. "I'm heading out. I promised to pick up a special sauce that Mandy needs for dinner tonight."

With a teasing glint in her eyes, she added, "If she needs it, you can be sure the trip to the store will be worth it."

Grinning, Alex agreed. "I'm sure it will be. Mandy's cooking rivals the best restaurants I've been to."

Stephanie continued. "I'll tell you all about it tomorrow and make your mouth water."

As she left his office, Alex endured a piercing sense of longing. Her presence had brightened his day, and her absence left him feeling incomplete.

CHAPTER TWELVE

AS STEPHANIE LEFT THE store with the newly purchased sauce in hand, she ventured back into the oncoming twilight. With the end of daylight savings time, the evenings stretched longer and brought a chill in the air that she was not accustomed to, being from Georgia.

Her thoughts drifted to the previous year when she'd spent evenings swimming in her apartment pool, enveloped in the fragrance of yellow azaleas amid the beauty of hollyhocks. The landscape in this area was a stark contrast, characterized by its rugged, rocky terrain, reminiscent of scenes from Western movies.

This time of peace had been a reprieve after the turbulent months she'd spent battling cancer, until chemotherapy had finally brought her hope. Now, with a clean bill of health, she had every reason to believe in a long and fulfilling life ahead.

However, the shadow of revealing her past illness to Alex loomed over her. She knew that life's uncertainties were a part of God's plan, as stated in the Bible. However, people often treated her differently when they learned about her previous struggle. She feared that Alex might react similarly.

Mandy had dinner almost ready when Stephanie returned home. She poured the sauce over the chicken and heated it before they sat down to eat.

During the meal, Mandy brought up plans to have dinner with Lissa and Jason the following Friday. "You're invited, dear. They'd really like for you to be there."

Stephanie cringed at the thought. The idea of being in the company of the blissful couple highlighted her own feelings of solitude. Still, she couldn't refuse Mandy's request. In a short time, she had grown to love and respect Mandy, and she didn't want to disappoint her.

She considered the invitation and asked, "Is there anything I can contribute for dinner?"

Mandy replied, "No, there's nothing we'll need. You'll be busy at work all day and I'm planning to make my famous coconut cake for dessert. I love baking. It's a treat for me."

Stephanie smiled and agreed. "I think it will be a treat for us as well."

The sauce was delicious and well worth a trip to the store. After they finished their dinner, Stephanie and Mandy worked together to clear the dishes. This was the part of the evening Stephanie enjoyed the most. It was during this time that Mandy often shared stories from her past or recounted events from the day. That evening, she told Stephanie about a visit to a new mother at the hospital. As she spoke about the newborn baby girl, her face lit up.

"The baby looks so much like her mother," Mandy remarked. "Seeing her brought back memories of when my granddaughters were babies. I used to stare at their beautiful faces for hours."

Stephanie sounded wistful. "I can imagine how precious they were to you. I don't have any babies in my family."

Mandy winked at her and said, "Someday, you will."

Those words stirred a deep ache in Stephanie's heart. She longed for Mandy's prediction to come true. However, the man who intrigued her the most was still mourning the loss of his wife. He wasn't looking for a new relationship, and that was a fact she had to accept.

Stephanie retired early. Her work was both demanding and fulfilling, often leaving her drained by the end of the day. She worked hard to maintain her professionalism and to try to keep her feelings for Alex at bay. However, the sight of him in the office the next morning would continue to challenge her resolve.

AS STEPHANIE SETTLED into her work the next day, she was focused on her tasks, primarily her ongoing projects. Alex entered the office. His words were straightforward as he inquired about the crew's progress on the Johnson project and the start of their work on the Foster project. Stephanie provided a thorough update, reflecting her commitment and enthusiasm for her job.

He then shifted his attention to her lunch plans. "Are you still going for a walk and lunch in the park today?"

Startled by the question, her pulse quickened as she replied, "Yes, I am. The weather is supposed to stay nice."

Alex smiled, his eyes warm and engaging. "Do you mind if Daniel and I join you for a picnic? I've got lunch for Daniel and myself, and I thought he'd love some outdoor time."

Stephanie hesitated, momentarily worried about the feelings that spending time with them could evoke. She had a genuine fondness for Daniel, and the prospect of forming a deeper bond with him and Alex was tempting. However, she was mindful of the delicate situation. Nevertheless, she agreed. "Sure, that sounds like a great idea. I'd love to see Daniel again."

Alex's eyes sparkled with appreciation, and he said, "Shall we plan to meet there around noon?"

"Sounds perfect. I'll bring my lunch, and we can go for a walk before eating."

As they discussed the details, Alex mentioned the contents of his picnic, including his bologna sandwich and a slightly bruised banana. Stephanie chuckled and offered to share some cookies Mandy had insisted she take. Their playful banter was a testament to the growing camaraderie between them.

With a parting laugh, he left her office to attend to his tasks, leaving Stephanie with a warm and contented feeling. She admired his unique blend of boyish charm and the confident, commanding presence he exuded.

Refocusing on her work, Stephanie diligently carried out her responsibilities. As noon approached, she prepared to leave for her lunchtime rendezvous at the park.

As she passed the reception desk, she noticed Linda's aloof demeanor as she said, "I understand you're going to the park with Alex and Daniel."

Stephanie perceived the underlying disapproval of her spending leisure time with Alex. She had already reassured Linda once that her relationship with Alex was purely professional, but Linda's cool manner persisted.

As Stephanie walked to the park she put Linda's disapproval out of her mind and enjoyed the crisp air of a cool front that had moved in. Though the desert sun offered some warmth, she shivered as the wind swept across her slacks and light sweater. Nevertheless, she continued towards the park, rubbing her hands together to warm them in the brisk weather.

Alex arrived soon afterward with Daniel, who squealed joyfully upon spying Stephanie. The little boy toddled across the grass to her and reached up, his arms outstretched.

She picked him up and beamed at him, saying, "I'm so glad to see you. too. Let's find a nice spot to enjoy our lunch."

Under the shade of an elm tree, they settled down, even though the day's crispness didn't require the shade's cover. Alex handed Daniel a half-sandwich and a bag of crackers. The little boy seemed most interested in the crackers and proceeded to munch on them with an occasional sip of juice.

Stephanie asked, "Is he always so selective about his food?"

Alex chuckled. "He has the strangest eating habits. One week, he'll only eat peanut butter, and the next, he might be all about fruits. I never know what he'll want."

"Kids can be quite unpredictable. I'm sure it's pretty normal for his age," Stephanie offered in assurance.

"I know, but I worry about his nutrition."

Stephanie praised him, saying, "Your concern just shows that you're a loving father. Otherwise, you wouldn't care so much."

"Thank you. I appreciate that. I don't always feel adequate as a parent."

Stephanie shared a bit about her own family, saying, "I was very close to my parents, even as a teenager. Though I was generally a good kid, they prayed for me a lot."

Alex looked at her curiously, saying, "I bet you were the type of kid who never got into real trouble."

"That's true. I never gave my parents any real reason to worry," she replied.

She asked about his own experiences and Alex confessed, "I went through a rebellious stage in my early teens. I snuck beers with my buddies and roamed the neighborhood with older friends after my parents went to sleep. But eventually, it lost its appeal, and I started making new friends in high school. I'm grateful that God turned me around before I got into any real trouble."

Stephanie empathized. "I have friends who are still dealing with the consequences of their teenage mistakes. I'm glad you changed course."

"Me, too! It set me on a different path, and I wouldn't have Daniel if I hadn't."

Daniel interrupted their conversation, exclaiming, "Play, Daddy!"

Alex decided to entertain him by swinging him in the park's baby swing. Daniel's laughter filled the air, and Stephanie smiled at the heartwarming sight.

After a few minutes of play, Alex lifted Daniel from the swing, and they walked along the path that led around the park. When they reached the turn leading back to the building, Daniel told Stephanie, "No. I stay with you!"

Stephanie's heart ached for the motherless child, but she gently declined. "I can't right now, honey. I have to go back to work."

When they reached the car, Alex lifted Daniel to put him into the car seat. The child clung to his father, not wanting to part from him. Stephanie admired Alex for his fatherly qualities. He was a dedicated and loving parent, and it touched her deeply.

"Maybe we can do this again," Stephanie assured Daniel before Alex closed the car door. She hoped she would have more opportunities to enjoy this little boy. Regrettably, now was not that time.

As they drove off, Stephanie made her way back to the office, feeling grateful for the quality time she had spent with Alex and Daniel.

When she walked into the office, she felt Linda's continued disapproval, evident by her silent reaction. Linda's apparent unease with Stephanie's interactions with Alex remained a concern even though Stephanie had made it clear that there was nothing more than friendship between them. What else could she do?

Later that afternoon, as she worked diligently on her projects, she overheard Alex's heated phone conversation. It became evident that an employee had stolen bedding materials meant for their projects. Stephanie sighed, knowing that such theft was an unfortunate issue in the landscaping industry. She would discuss the repercussions with Alex when he was ready.

Chapter Thirteen

THE NEXT MORNING, STEPHANIE arrived at the office, her thoughts filled with curiosity about whether Alex had managed to resolve the issue with his thieving employee. Though Linda had been absent in the reception area, Alex was already in his office, gazing out of the window with a scowl on his face.

Stephanie settled into her workspace, placing her purse behind her desk, and switching on her computer. After a moment's hesitation, she decided to approach Alex to discuss the theft.

Knocking on his open office door, Stephanie asked, "I overheard a bit of what happened yesterday. Do you want to talk about it?"

Alex let out a sigh as he ran his fingers through his hair and motioned for her to come in. The chair in front of his desk was comfortably overstuffed for customers, but Stephanie felt a bit uneasy in his office, especially with his current mood, which made her feel like she was sitting in the principal's office.

"I've put a lot of effort into building this business to where it is today," Alex began, his voice tinged with frustration. "And this guy didn't just steal materials. He stole profits I've earned through countless sleepless nights designing, days supervising jobs under the scorching sun, and personal sacrifices to funnel money back into the company."

Stephanie chimed in. "The irony is that he'd feel just as angry if someone stole from him."

Alex nodded, acknowledging the point. "Exactly. He most likely rationalized his actions."

"The Golden Rule seems to be for everyone else," Stephanie commented wryly.

Alex grimaced, his expression darkening, "Precisely. Now he'll probably move on to another place and do the same thing again. He's probably done it before. I was too furious to fire him in person, so I had Rob take care of it."

Stephanie inquired, "Are you considering pressing charges against him?"

Alex sighed in response. "I don't have concrete evidence. Rob caught him with the stolen supplies in his truck, but he argued that they couldn't fit in the company's truck."

Stephanie questioned further. "Could they have fit?"

"Yes, they could have! Besides, we could have used a pickup truck for the rest." Alex's voice held frustration.

"Since you're understandably angry, it was probably for the best that you had someone else handle it," Stephanie suggested. "Just remember that if he continues to steal, he's bound to get caught, and likely, he'll end up serving jail time."

Alex sighed, conceding. "You're right. I need to let this go. There are more important things to worry about."

Stephanie agreed. "That's true. You need to go over the plans with me for my latest project. I believe I've covered all the details, but I'd appreciate your input."

As they discussed the project details, Stephanie noticed the scent of Alex's cologne, a mild citrusy fragrance that added to the warmth of their conversation. She managed to keep her mind on the business at hand but couldn't keep her thoughts from wandering back to the qualities she admired in Alex. He was industrious, intelligent, kind, and responsible, loving to Danile, not to mention handsome.

Her focus snapped back to reality when Alex mentioned, "I believe with the adjustments we just made, it's ready to go."

Stephanie nodded and replied, "Yes, thanks to Rob for returning the stolen materials in the truck. I plan to spend the day personally overseeing the job and making revisions to the plans for the next one.

I'll check with you before ordering any new supplies. If all goes as planned, we can start the new project next week."

With a friendly gesture, Alex placed his hand on Stephanie's arm. Her body reacted to his touch with an electrifying tremor, and she met his gaze as he spoke, "I still owe you that dinner for the evening you watched Daniel for me. Can we go tomorrow? There's a great Mexican restaurant nearby if you'd like that."

Stephanie grappled with inner conflict. Her rational side told her to make an excuse to maintain professionalism, as her feelings for Alex were growing stronger. Yet, heart overruled, and she simply couldn't help but accept his offer. "Sure, I do enjoy Mexican food."

Alex's eyes sparkled as he suggested, "We can touch base tomorrow to decide on a time."

"That sounds perfect," Stephanie replied. "In the meantime, if we're finished for today, I'll go home to see what Mandy has prepared for dinner."

Alex agreed. "We're done for now. I'll be heading home in a few minutes. I'll see you tomorrow."

As Stephanie made her way to her car, a whirlwind of thoughts raced through her mind. She fought the temptation to read too much into Alex's invitation, though she couldn't help wondering how he felt about her. Perhaps it was just a simple gesture of gratitude for her help with Daniel.

UPON ARRIVING AT MANDY'S house, Stephanie found that Lissa was just leaving. They chatted briefly in the foyer, where Lissa shared her excitement about her pregnancy and her plans for the nursery.

"We just got back from running to the mall. I found out today our baby is a little 'Miss.' Grandma's helping me pick out décor for the nursery. Jason and I painted the room a soft turquoise because we both like the color. Now I can accent it with pink."

Stephanie hugged her and expressed her happiness for her friend. She knew that Mandy had surely enjoyed their shopping trip for baby items, and it warmed her heart to see Lissa and Mandy bonding over this special time.

"Grandma's in the kitchen. I try not to let her overdo it, but she's hard to slow down," Lissa said.

"I'll check on her," Stephanie said. "And I'll take care of doing the dishes and wiping up after supper."

Lissa was grateful for Stephanie's presence, stating, "I'm glad you're here with her."

A cool breeze swept into the foyer when Lissa departed, and Stephanie quickly moved into the warm heart of the house. She passed through the dimly lit parlor and entered the kitchen. Mandy was carrying a bowl of hot biscuits to the table, and the delightful aroma filled the air.

"I've made a tuna casserole to go with these," Mandy mentioned with a warm smile.

The scent of the freshly baked biscuits, butter, and jam all on the table made Stephanie's mouth water. The idea of butter melting into the fluffy biscuits with the jam was particularly tempting.

Stephanie quickly washed her hands and joined Mandy at the table, where they dug into the casserole. The warm, comforting flavors filled the room, and Stephanie noted, "This is what I call comfort food."

Mandy smiled, "I'm glad you like it. I didn't have much time to prepare anything more elaborate."

"You don't need to make elaborate meals for me. I love simple foods."

As they continued eating, Stephanie thought about her own longing to have a child. The topic of family and babies had been a sensitive one for her, and Mandy's excitement about her upcoming great-grandchild stirred up her own desires.

Changing the subject, she mused, "I could pick up a dessert for Friday night with Lissa and her husband. What do they like?"

Mandy replied, "Chocolate. They both love chocolate cream pie or chocolate cake. I'll let Lissa know about your offer."

Once they had finished their meal, Stephanie guided Mandy into the living room and suggested they find a light comedy show to watch. While Mandy was occupied with the remote control, Stephanie cleared the table and started loading the dishes into the dishwasher.

As Stephanie went about her task, her thoughts kept returning to her dinner plans with Alex for the next day. She felt torn between the desire to spend time with him and the fear that an intimate outing could intensify the budding romantic attraction that was building. However, she knew she couldn't back out now.

IN HIS HOME, ALEX GENTLY rubbed the back of his sleeping son, the soft light from the hall casting a warm glow on the little boy's face. Memories of Kelly, the excitement of expecting a son, and their shared dreams filled his mind as he pondered his current situation. He had once believed he could never love anyone again, but the thought of Stephanie had started to chip away at that conviction.

He wondered if his desire to get closer to Stephanie was simply a response to his loneliness. Kelly would have wanted him to move on and find happiness, yet he still felt guilty about it. His late wife's memory weighed heavily on his heart, and the pain of her loss was a constant presence.

He tried to manage his conflicting emotions and remind himself to tread carefully. Stephanie had proved that she was a kind-hearted and good-natured woman, and a valuable part of his team. As he watched

Daniel sleep, he acknowledged that she had been a blessing, but he wasn't sure if he was ready to move forward.

It was clear that their relationship was transitioning from a professional one to something deeper, yet Alex couldn't deny the chemistry he felt when he was with Stephanie. He couldn't help but be drawn to her and the way she made him forget his past pain.

As he considered the upcoming dinner date with Stephanie, he knew that he couldn't make any assumptions about her intentions. Could she have any romantic interest in him, or was their connection purely friendly and professional? He needed answers to these questions, and their dinner the next evening would be the perfect opportunity.

He hoped it would be a chance for open and honest conversation. He wondered if Stephanie harbored feelings for anyone else. Were there past romances that he didn't know about? His emotions were tangled in the delicate threads of attraction, caution, and the enduring love he held for his late wife.

As he glanced at the clock, he realized he was running late to work due to Daniel's slow start in the morning. He didn't want his delayed start to cause him to get behind in his work and miss their routine lunch in the park. He knew how much Daniel looked forward to this outing. For now, he decided to prioritize what he wanted, and he was determined not to cancel their lunch plans.

When Alex arrived at work and saw Linda, he told her, "I'm going to grab a cup of coffee and go over some plans with Stephanie."

Linda's gaze narrowed, "You've given her a lot of responsibility. I hope she's not learning the ropes just to open her own firm and leave you."

Alex didn't like the idea of Stephanie moving on after she had become such a valuable asset in such a short time to his business. He inquired, "Has she mentioned anything like that to you?"

Linda reassured him. "No, not at all. It's just that she seems very ambitious."

Alex sighed, acknowledging his concern. "I don't think she plans on leaving anytime soon. She hasn't given any indication, but I can't force her to promise to stay."

Linda offered another perspective. "It might not be her leaving that you should worry about the most. She's a pleasant and attractive woman. What if she's trying to win your affection to become a part owner of the firm? Kelly and I were close friends, and she'd want me to warn you to be careful."

Alex felt a twinge of discomfort at Linda's suggestion, and he bristled at the insinuations. Stephanie was nothing but a dedicated and hardworking employee, and he had no reason to suspect her of any ulterior motives. He resolved to enjoy their upcoming dinner and get to know her better outside the office.

THE DAY WENT BY, AND before they knew it, it was time for lunch. As Alex entered Stephanie's office, she greeted him with a warm smile. "I've been working on some plans, and I think I've come up with something that will work."

The conversation flowed effortlessly as they discussed the project details. With each moment they spent together, the scent of lavender and Stephanie's warm presence filled the room. Her proximity sent Alex's heart racing, and he couldn't help but be captivated by her charm and beauty.

As their conversation came to an end, Stephanie hesitated for a moment and fixed Alex with her dark, expressive eyes. "Mandy will be away for a week before Mother's Day," she shared. "When she returns, I'd like to surprise her with a collection of phalaenopsis orchids. Could I order them through the business to get a discount?"

Alex thought it was a great idea and agreed. "Certainly. We can include them in our next order of foliage."

Her eyes sparkled with appreciation as she thanked him. "That will save me at least fifty dollars for three plants. Mandy fell in love with the purple and pink ones in the grocery store, but they were too expensive."

Stephanie added, "I'm glad she has time to take care of her plants. She enjoys them and also keeps busy with her volunteer work at the church. Last week, she helped with meals for shut-ins and the elderly."

As they discussed the church and their Sunday attendance, Alex found himself battling a pang of jealousy when he pondered Stephanie's connection with the other churchgoers, especially the single men. He couldn't help but wonder if any of them had made advances or if she had an interest in someone else. He sighed, knowing he had no right to claim any part of her life.

When he mentioned attending Sunday school, he was surprised by his own words. It was an unexpected commitment, but he considered it a step toward spending more time with Stephanie. Their shared ride to church would allow him to get to know her better and discover more about her personal life.

Stephanie's thoughts were on her own desires, particularly her wish for a family, which was in stark contrast to Linda's warnings. As the conversation flowed, she couldn't help but think about Alex and how he could fit into her future. The temptation to be with him was growing stronger, and she realized that she couldn't back out of their dinner plans now.

THE ALLURE OF MEXICAN food beckoned, when they headed to Alex's favorite restaurant, with its vibrant exterior painted with red chilies. As Stephanie joked about trying "the hard stuff," Alex recommended some of his favorite dishes. When he mentioned sopapillas, a delicious, deep-fried pastry, Stephanie's curiosity was piqued.

As they settled into their booth by the window, Stephanie was struck by the lovely view of the river and the geese that graced its surface. The atmosphere of the restaurant felt welcoming and homey to her, much like the small-town cafés she admired.

Their dinner conversation flowed easily, with Stephanie and Alex sharing their love of good food and acknowledging their shared enjoyment in dining out. The exchange was light and friendly, with Alex joking about a possible cut of the restaurant's profits for his recommendations.

The dinner was enjoyable, and both Stephanie and Alex found themselves looking forward to more of these casual outings. However, each of them was haunted by their own uncertainties and desires, which they couldn't easily reveal to the other.

As their dinner came to an end, Alex felt a mix of anticipation and trepidation about where his feelings for Stephanie were headed.

Chapter Fourteen

ALEX SETTLED THE TAB, and they drove down Main Street under the setting sun. Stephanie gazed out of the window, her voice filled with contentment. "I haven't been here long, but I've fallen in love with the cloudless blue sky, the rosy mesas, and the stunning sunsets."

"Ever miss the abundant green foliage and the variety of trees from back east?" Alex asked, his eyes darting from the road to her.

As she peered out in search of eagles that reportedly nested in the live oaks by the river, Stephanie answered thoughtfully, "Sometimes I miss the greens and being closer to the ocean. But I've fallen in love with this land. It's rugged and powerful. It has character."

Pulling into Mandy's driveway, Alex nodded with a grin. "Spoken like a true landscape architect. We appreciate the beauty of nature."

Stephanie chuckled. "Yet, we're always trying to change it."

"For the better, of course," he added, pointing to the medians along the street. "See the flowers there? They bloom all summer."

As he walked her to the door, Stephanie's heart raced. She didn't expect him to kiss her. Nonetheless, she hoped it wouldn't be an awkward parting.

She found her key and turned to face him. The dinner was delicious. Thank you for the treat."

"You've more than earned it," he said.

With a smile and a nod, he added, "I'll see you in the morning."

Then he turned and walked away.

Relieved, Stephanie entered the foyer. Though she hadn't wanted an awkward parting, part of her had yearned for the kiss.

THE NEXT MORNING, ALEX arrived right behind Stephanie, and they walked into the building together. Linda shot them a disapproving look, raising an eyebrow in apparent judgment. While Alex didn't seem to notice, Linda's lack of trust continued to baffle Stephanie.

"Did I miss any calls?" he asked.

Linda waved a sheet of paper at him. "A couple of important ones. The doctor and his wife want you to come to their barbecue on the patio you designed for them. And the bricklayers for the Anderson project ran into a delay getting the replacements delivered."

Alex sighed, "Another headache. I'll call our head foreman about the bricks. They are a special pattern."

As they parted ways for their offices, Stephanie dwelt on how much she had enjoyed their dinner at a restaurant last night. It wasn't a date, but they had connected on a deep, emotional level, sharing many interests. She couldn't shake the feeling that perhaps it was all in her imagination. She decided it was wiser to assume that Alex felt nothing of what she was feeling. Getting her hopes up, only to have them dashed by reality. was a scenario she wished to avoid at all costs.

ON FRIDAY AFTERNOON, Stephanie was closing her office when she saw Alex preparing to leave. "Daniel will be glad it's the weekend, so he can spend time with you," she remarked.

Alex grinned. "We're going to put on cartoons tonight and eat pizza. How about you?"

"Mandy and I are going over to Lissa and Jason's house for supper. I'm a little nervous. I'm not a very good socialite."

He chuckled. "I wouldn't worry about it. I think Mandy has that covered."

"You're right. She's friendly enough for both of us."

He accompanied her down the hall and continued, "I'm sure you'll have a good time."

"I will, but I don't know them very well."

"If you skip out early, you can come to watch cartoons."

Stephanie shot him a glance, surprised by his suggestion.

He gave her a wry grin. "It doesn't sound like a stimulating evening, does it?"

"It sounds like you're a good father and plan to have fun with your little boy."

"Thanks. I treasure every minute with him, although I have to admit I've forgotten what grown-ups do for fun."

Stephanie saw a deep longing in his eyes for what he had lost when Kelly was no longer there as a companion. She imagined his evenings were long after Daniel went to bed, and he had no one to share them with. At least she had Mandy to talk to about her day.

After stopping at the grocery store to pick up a chocolate cream pie to contribute to the evening meal, she went home to freshen up. The house was filled with a wonderful aroma.

"Have you been baking bread?" she asked Mandy, following her nose to the kitchen.

Mandy looked up from her crossword puzzle, greeted Stephanie with a smile, and replied, "Since I wasn't making our supper tonight, I decided it would be a good day to bake a few loaves. I'll take one over for supper tonight and freeze the others."

Four butter-topped brown mounds were cooling on racks on the counter, and Stephanie's stomach rumbled at the sight, begging her for a slice slathered in butter and strawberry jam.

"This looks delicious," she told Mandy.

"It will go well with whatever Lissa is making. She's gotten to be a very good cook."

"She learned from you, I believe," Stephanie said.

Mandy smiled. "We may have worked on a few recipes together. We share recipes when we find new ones that look good."

Stephanie wondered what it would be like to spend an afternoon in the kitchen with Mandy. She thought of the times she'd made desserts with her mom. "Though I've never cooked a full meal for a family, I've made lots of treats. I'd love to have the ability you have."

"Do you have plans for Easter?" Mandy asked.

Stephanie shook her head. "No. I won't have time to fly home."

"Do you want to spend it with us at Lissa and Jason's house? I'm making ham as the main course, and Lissa is providing plates and silverware. I could use help in the kitchen."

"I'd love to, if you're sure it would be all right with Lissa and Jason."

"I'll talk to Lissa, but I'm sure she'd love to have you come."

"If so, I'll finally learn how to bake a ham."

They took the bread and the chocolate cream pie in Mandy's car and headed to dinner with Lissa and Jason. They parked along the sidewalk and walked the path to the ornate gate. Unlocking it, they walked to the house. From a well-lit foyer, they made their way into the dining room and kitchen area, where Jason was pouring water into glasses.

"I hope you're hungry. Lissa made enough food to feed a family of ten," he announced.

"I'm sure we can help you with that," Mandy replied.

"Should I put dessert in the kitchen?" Stephanie asked.

"Let me have a look first. I might have a better use for it," Jason said.

Mandy pointed a finger at him, saying, "No dessert until you clean your plate."

"I'm afraid I do that all too often. Lissa's a good cook."

"Is that my darling grandmother?" Lissa called from the kitchen.

Mandy said with a chuckle, "I'll answer to that."

Lissa smiled at them from behind the counter that separated the dining room from the kitchen. "You can set the bread and dessert here. I'm almost finished."

They complied with her request and as Lissa breathed in the yeasty scent of the bread, she commented, "That smells wonderful. Make yourselves at home while I take the roast from the oven."

"Nonsense. I want to help," Mandy said, marching into the kitchen and unwrapping the plastic wrap from the bread, slicing the loaf into uniform pieces.

Stephanie asked, "What can I do?"

Lissa quickly decided. "You can toss the salad and set it on the table."

Stephanie glanced around the tidy little kitchen, admiring the decor. "The color coordination in your kitchen might make me think an artist lives here."

Lissa grinned. "I was impressed with this place the minute I saw it. Besides the decor, Jason's unbelievably neat. I couldn't believe a single guy lived here."

"That must be nice for you. Most women complain their husbands leave dirty clothes all over the floor."

"Not Jason. Compared to him, I'm the messy one."

"She lived with me, and she was never untidy," Mandy said.

"I wasn't pregnant then. My energy is so low. I can't keep up with housework as well as I usually do."

"That's understandable," Mandy said. "You seem to be feeling well now."

"Finally. In a couple of months, I hear my nesting instinct will kick in. I'll clean like crazy and get everything ready for the baby."

Mandy gave her a gentle hug. "That's how it happened for me."

Stephanie felt left out of the conversation, pondering whether or not, one day, she would be qualified to compare notes on impending motherhood with Lissa and Mandy. Mandy would be an excellent source of advice about child-rearing.

Jason wandered into the kitchen. "We're ready out there."

Lissa said, "The roasted potatoes and salad are done. So, we're good to go."

He kissed her on the neck and leaned past her to sniff the bread. "Smells good."

Lissa chuckled. "Me or the food?"

"Both."

They all filled their plates with roast, mashed potatoes smothered in rich brown gravy, the colorful salad, and Mandy's freshly baked bread. Seated at the table, Jason led the prayer, and they echoed his "Amen" before heartily diving into the meal.

"This is delicious," Stephanie said.

"Thanks. You'll never guess where I got the recipe," Lissa said.

Stephanie nodded toward Mandy. "I think I know."

"My mother didn't cook much when I was growing up. Grandma Mandy taught me all I know," Lissa admitted.

"That was an advantage for me," Jason added.

They continued their conversation, delving into their families and the adjustments they had made to living in a small southwestern city after growing up farther east.

"Do you miss the city?" Stephanie asked Lissa.

"Not at all. I miss my parents, my sister and her husband, and their baby. But I don't miss the traffic, crime, or the humidity. I've come to love the shades of brown in the high desert."

"It's growing on me, too," Stephanie admitted.

"How's your job going?" Jason inquired.

"It's wonderful. The challenge of finding desert plants and those suited for this climate has broadened my design ability. There are hundreds of choices of foliage for warm, humid climates. Here, not so much."

"You seem to be hitting it off well with Alex," Lissa said, her intent unclear, though Stephanie hoped she wasn't alluding to a budding romance.

Stephanie chose to address the professional aspect. "He's a great boss. He gives me lots of leeway to draw up designs for my clients. I'm also working on expanding the business to southwestern Colorado. I think there's real potential there."

"That's wonderful. With your help, he could grow his company," Lissa noted.

The conversation shifted towards their shared enthusiasm for Alex's success, a topic that allowed Stephanie to avoid the inner turmoil regarding her personal feelings for him.

During dessert, the conversation turned to baby names as they brainstormed suggestions for Lissa and Jason's baby girl. Stephanie felt somewhat awkward suggesting a name for people she hardly knew. When it was her turn to chime in, she offered, "I've always liked Bethany Ann."

Lissa tried it out. "I like that. It rolls off my tongue smoothly. We'll keep all the suggestions in mind."

"Whatever you name her, we'll love her dearly," Mandy assured.

Lissa smiled. "I know. She's a fortunate girl."

They continued to chat about their plans for Easter, and Lissa and Jason were eager to have Stephanie join them.

"I have an old family recipe for pecan pie. I could bring one, along with whatever else you'd like," Stephanie offered.

"The pie sounds wonderful. Bring it," Lissa said.

"How about a relish tray, too? I like doing those," Stephanie suggested.

"I'd like that," Jason said. "I need to nibble before the meal. The smell of ham makes me hungry."

"All right. Bring on the pickles and celery. It doesn't dull his appetite for the meal," Lissa teased. "He'll happily eat turkey or ham for a week after Thanksgiving, Christmas, and Easter, anyway."

"That's nice for getting rid of leftovers," Stephanie pointed out.

"I sound like a disposal," Jason joked.

As they shared a laugh, Lissa remarked, "I'm fortunate to have a guy who's not picky about his food."

Mandy winked at her, saying, "I was right about you two, wasn't I?"

Lissa sighed. "You were right and I'm grateful."

They helped Lissa clean the kitchen before sitting down to play a game of Spades. Although it was new to Stephanie, she quickly caught on, helping her partner, Mandy, win.

"I hate to win and run, but it's getting late for this senior citizen," Mandy said when the game was over.

"Yet, you do like to win," Lissa observed with a grin.

"Indeed, I do."

Mandy kissed Lissa goodbye, and they walked into the still, silent night. The stars sparkled like a dazzling necklace around the pale face of the moon, and Stephanie shivered, longing for the warmth of her blankets. Tomorrow, she would sleep in before catching up with laundry and chores.

"Lissa didn't think she and Jason had much in common. But I knew those two were made for each other," Mandy said.

"How long did it take for them to realize it?"

"A few months," Mandy recalled.

"They seem so happy," Stephanie commented.

"Yes, they are. Lissa is more content than I've ever seen her. They're opposites in many ways, but it worked out well.."

After a few moments of silence, Mandy asked, "Alex didn't come to your Sunday school last week, did he?"

"No. He left after the church service," Stephanie replied.

"Why? Didn't he like it?"

Stephanie sighed. "I don't know. He said he thought Daniel was coming down with a cold."

Mandy's mention of Alex, after discussing Lissa and Jason's happiness, made Stephanie wonder if she were trying to be a matchmaker once again.

In an effort to change the subject, Stephanie asked, "How did you and your husband meet?"

Mandy shared, "I was clerking in a small drugstore. He broke his ankle on the job and came in for crutches. I fitted him. The rest is history."

"That's romantic."

"Sometimes romance needs help. I gave him a call to see how the crutches were working out. We chatted for a while, and he asked me out."

"That was crafty of you."

Stephanie and Mandy pulled into the two-car garage, the chatter about Mandy's matchmaking tactics still fresh in their minds. The engine was silenced, and they were enveloped in the quiet of the garage. Mandy, her face reflecting a mix of curiosity and mischief, turned to Stephanie. With a knowing glint in her eyes, Mandy remarked, "I bet several young men have fallen hard for you."

The innocent remark triggered a bittersweet memory for Stephanie. She replied with a hint of sadness. "I was engaged once. He broke it off after I got sick."

Mandy furrowed her brows in genuine concern, sympathy shining in her eyes. "You must have been very ill."

Stephanie elaborated, "I had non-Hodgkin's lymphoma. The jury was out on whether or not I'd survive treatment and live."

Mandy's face exuded warmth as she expressed her empathy. "I'm so sorry, dear. I didn't know. You look well now."

"I am," Stephanie reassured her, a glimmer of gratitude in her eyes. "I was diagnosed over five years ago, and the doctors don't expect it to come back. Of course, there's no guarantee."

Mandy nodded thoughtfully, her empathy still evident. "I'm glad to hear your prognosis is good. You must have had a challenging time juggling illness, a job, and an engagement."

Stephanie's thoughts delved back into the past, remembering the difficult choices she'd had to make during her treatment. "It was hard not having Neal's support. Still, it was better to find out then than later that he wouldn't stick by me."

As she spoke, Stephanie's mind drifted to Alex, to his history with Kelly, and the loss he'd endured. She wondered if he would be willing to take a chance on a cancer survivor, even though she had been cured. The thought of seeing pity in his eyes, the typical response, was something she wanted to avoid at all costs.

Chapter Fifteen

ALEX WALKED INTO THE building, clutching a steaming mug of coffee, the weariness of a long night with Daniel etched on his face. Daniel had been plagued by a nightmare involving an alligator from a picture book he'd seen at the sitter's house. That morning, Alex had made a point of asking the sitter to remove the book from her shelves. His thoughts, however, were also plagued by Linda's insinuations about Stephanie.

As he walked down the corridor, the unsettling idea that Stephanie might be working hard to infiltrate a partnership gnawed at him. Determinedly, he tried to bury this unwelcome notion deep within his mind, locking it away until he had any concrete reasons to confront it.

In his office, he delved into work, focusing on the final details of a corporate project. When Stephanie arrived, he called her in for a meeting, finding solace in her sweet smile and morning greeting.

"Did you have a good weekend?" she asked.

Alex replied, "Mostly. Saturday was filled with chores. As you know, on Sunday, we missed church because Daniel had a runny nose. When he felt better, we took a walk and watched a kid movie before we fell asleep on the couch. Then everything was okay until during the night when Daniel was awake for an hour with a bad dream."

Stephanie's sympathy shone through as she inquired, "Oh, that's hard. I bet you're tired. Do you need a refill on the coffee?"

"No, I'm good. Thanks," he replied. If Stephanie's kindness was an act, she was remarkably convincing.

He tapped the screen to show her a three-stage mall landscaping project he was working on. "I want your initial reaction to this. Is there anything you would change?"

She studied the design and appreciated the use of knolls to create a park-like setting, covering the parking lot behind the food court. Her perceptive suggestion about adding a playground and considering the possibility of a daycare drew his attention.

"That's a clever idea. I'll mention it to mall management," Alex acknowledged, pleased with her insights.

"I don't see anything else I'd change," Stephanie said.

"I'm taking it over to them at ten o'clock. We'll see what they say," he said, looking forward to the client meeting.

"Speaking of designs," Stephanie interjected, "I found out that we have a green light to begin planning the subdivision in Colorado. We can put in trees and a park with a hiking area. This will look good on the job portfolio. Word of mouth should get us more projects in the area."

Alex, eyebrows raised, teased, "You're going to get more work than we can do if you keep this up."

With a chuckle, Stephanie replied, "You'll have to expand and employ an additional designer."

Amid Stephanie's enthusiasm, Alex's mind briefly revisited Linda's words. Was Stephanie attempting to assert herself to his equal in the company, as suggested by Linda? He decided to rein in his reservations, cautioning, "Let's take it one job at a time."

Stephanie bit her lip, her uncertainty evident, and Alex sensed her puzzlement. He couldn't explain the source of his hesitation. He simply hoped Linda was wrong. In the meantime, he didn't want to risk hurting Stephanie's feelings or damaging the potential for a future relationship.

"We're finished here. I'll let you get back to work. Thanks for your input," he concluded.

"Sure. That's my job," Stephanie replied, her disquiet still lingering. With no further words to share, he let her return to her work.

By afternoon, he had talked himself out of believing Stephanie had ulterior motives in the company. Everything seemed to be falling back into place. He decided to confront his fears and suspicions head on.

Later in the afternoon, he visited Stephanie in her office, expressing his gratitude. "I appreciated your help this morning."

She offered a half-smile, conceding, "I didn't mean to push too hard about expanding. I'll slow down."

"Just let me catch my breath," he responded, giving her an understanding nod.

"It's a deal," she agreed, visibly relieved as her smile widened.

"I'm taking Daniel to the park for lunch tomorrow," he said. "Would you like to join us?"

"Sure. I'll jog while you pick him up and then have lunch with you two."

The prospect of having her with them the next day brought a genuine smile to Alex's face. They wouldn't discuss business. They would just enjoy each other's company, and, for once, not worry about what the future might hold.

As he tucked Daniel into bed, reading a story from his children's Bible, he contemplated how different things might have been if Kelly were still here. His thoughts, which usually drifted towards work after putting Daniel to bed, found their way to a moment of quiet reflection.

THE NEXT MORNING BROUGHT with it light rain and overcast skies. He fed Daniel, dishing out scrambled eggs and oatmeal, though the little boy pushed the food away with a frown.

"What's up? You like eggs and oatmeal," Alex said, puzzled. "Take a bite."

Encouraging Daniel to eat a few more bites, he finally got the little boy to comply, and Alex served juice. It wasn't an ideal start to the day, but Alex was determined to salvage it with their planned lunch at the park.

The next morning, after picking up Daniel, he couldn't suppress a pang of guilt after buying his son yet another burger for supper, straying from his commitment to provide healthier meals. He silently vowed to return to his usual cooking routine soon.

After a busy morning, the skies cleared by the time Alex picked up Daniel for their picnic with Stephanie. Watching her cradle Daniel in her arms, Alex realized that it was the maternal affection Daniel missed. Alex worried that the child would miss her if her job eventually took her to another city.

Nonetheless, their picnic provided a temporary escape from these somber thoughts. As they played and laughed together, Alex felt a profound sense of gratitude for Stephanie's presence, even if it was only for this moment. They climbed the fort, took turns on the slide, and allowed Daniel to enjoy the simple pleasures of childhood.

However, as the day progressed, the fear of Stephanie leaving someday loomed large in Alex's mind. He couldn't shake the feeling that their connection was growing stronger, yet he also knew that it was essential to tread cautiously.

As they shared their meals, Alex briefly escaped the burden of his worries. As they conversed, Alex learned more about Stephanie's interests and her past, feeling a connection that went beyond mere attraction.

Their conversation turned to their childhoods, and as Alex shared his memories of being a quiet child who loved reading and math, Stephanie recounted her own experiences in ballet, singing in the school choir, and her love for outdoor activities. Their exchange made him appreciate her even more, a unique blend of ambition, perseverance, and sweetness.

As he was thinking about her happy childhood, she playfully questioned, "With all the money you'll soon be making, do you think we could have caviar in the break room?"

Alex chuckled,. "Not with the rent I'm paying."

Stephanie's mischievous smile left him intrigued. Alex pondered the ongoing changes in their dynamics, wondering if there would be an even deeper connection they were forging. He was determined to take it one step at a time, as he didn't want to jeopardize the future of the company or their personal relationship.

Their time at the park concluded with more play, making Daniel's day brighter. When it was time to leave, the sprinkles of rain began again. Though Daniel protested, Stephanie sang a nursery rhyme to provide a soothing reassurance to the little boy.

As he dropped Stephanie at the office, Alex couldn't shake the melancholy that had taken hold of him. He knew he had to be cautious with his growing emotions, especially when it came to Daniel's attachment to her. The uncertainty of Stephanie's future weighed heavily on him, and he couldn't afford to let his feelings run rampant.

That evening, as the rain fell and he settled into bed with his book, he found himself caught between the past and an uncertain future. His thoughts raced, but his emotions remained guarded. He had embarked on an unexpected journey, one that brought moments of joy, but he couldn't deny the challenges and uncertainties that lay ahead.

Chapter Sixteen

STEPHANIE JOGGED THROUGH fat drops of chilly rain on the way back to the office. It was only across the park lawn and parking lot, but she was chilled when she arrived. She ditched her damp sneakers and donned the low heels she had worn to work.

The sky had turned a dismal gray and a puddle of rain drizzled down her window like icing on hot cinnamon bread. She shivered. After having fun in the park, loneliness settled over like a thick fog.

Though she loved coming home to Mandy, she continued to wonder what it would be like to have a family, a husband, and children to care for. She shook off the thoughts as Linda arrived to drop off her mail.

"You have a registered letter that needs a signature," Linda said.

Stephanie accepted the letter. "Thanks. I've been waiting for this. "She signed and handed the slip back to Linda. "Could you come back after you deliver the slip to the postal carrier?"

"Sure. I'll be right back." Linda shot her a curious look.

It was rare for Stephanie to summon Linda to her office. Stephanie wasn't sure she knew what she was going to say, but she knew it was time to talk.

When Linda returned, Stephanie asked her to sit. Taking a deep breath to summon courage, Stephanie said, "I know you were good friends with Kelly. I'm not trying to take her place with either you or Alex. I'd like us to be friends, too."

Linda's eyes widened, as though surprised by Stephanie's forthrightness. Gaining composure, she said, "You've spent personal time with Alex. What am I supposed to think? You win his heart, get him to marry you, and you get an interest in his company. You don't have to build one from the ground up."

"I'd never use marriage to advance a career! The personal cost would be too high. If I marry, it will be because I fall in love and have found the person God has planned for me."

"I want to believe you. Still, you must understand I don't want to see Alex get heartbroken again. It's taken him this long to get back on his feet after losing Kelly."

"I understand your mistrust. I can assure you I have no plans to get personally involved with Alex."

"You're attracted to him, aren't you?"

Stephanie hesitated, not sure she was obligated to share her feelings with someone already suspicious of her motives. Yet, since she had nothing to hide, she decided to answer. "I am, but I don't plan to act on it. Office relationships are best kept professional."

"I agree. It makes me feel better to find you understand the dangers of being less than professional."

"That doesn't mean co-workers can't be friends. That's all it's been when we've met at the park to have lunch with Daniel."

Linda raised her brows, looking skeptical. "I guess we'll see. I better get back to work."

Stephanie sighed as she watched her walk from the room. How could she convince this woman she wasn't trying to steal the company? Perhaps, given time, Linda would believe her. As to Stephanie's feelings for Alex, that was another question.

She pushed the unresolved issue with Linda to the back of her mind as she tweaked the three-dimensional model pulled up on her computer. She heard Alex's footsteps in the hallway. He paused at his doorway and shrugged off the black overcoat that made him look like a dashing undercover agent.

He shut the door when he went into his office. Forcing her mind back to her computer, she finished her task by late afternoon. She drove home and found Mandy making a baby quilt for a December birth.

"I haven't been out today," Mandy said. "Is it cold?"

"Chilly. The temperatures are in the forties. It feels good in the house. Smells good, too."

"I started our stew. Cornbread and cherry cobbler are on the menu, too," Mandy said.

"That sounds wonderful. It's hearty for a cool spring night. It looks like the quilt is almost finished."

"It is. This sweet baby boy will be warm if I have anything to say about it. If I finish it tomorrow, I can start planning Easter dinner. Remember, you're coming with me. Lissa wants you there."

"I am. I appreciate being invited."

"Alex and Daniel are invited, too. He usually has Easter with his brother and Linda. This year they're going to be out of town with her family."

Stephanie tried to hide her uncertainty with a quick response. "Of course. The more the better. Just let me pitch in with the work. I don't cook a lot, but I'd love to help an expert. I could learn more than how to make one kind of pie or how to put together a relish tray."

"That's an overstatement. I'm hardly a five-star chef. I do make a mean ham and a great potato salad, though. Except for pies and potato salad, we'll be cooking at Lissa's. It's easier than making things here and carrying them over."

"What time does it all need to be ready?"

Though she used to love the sunrise service, the idea of rising at dawn to put in the ham didn't appeal to Stephanie. However, she was determined to be a good sport. These people were offering her company and feeding her a meal. It was the least she could do.

"I'll go over at seven o'clock and start the ham. We can finish the other preparations after church. We eat at about noon. That gives us plenty of time to get things done."

Stephanie's thoughts drifted to past Easters. "I used to love going to the sunrise Easter service as a kid. Then, we'd come home, and I'd hunt eggs. Later, I'd sit down with my parents, and we'd have Mom's dinner. If the weather was nice afterward, we'd bundle up and go to the park down the block. I'd play on the playground while my parents sat on a bench and chatted. When I got older, we switched to games of croquet and badminton in the backyard."

"You're lucky to have good holiday memories. In some households, it's a time of stress and bickering. I know a few folks at church who don't look forward to getting together with their relatives each year," Mandy said.

"I know and that is sad. I'm going to miss my parents."

Mandy smiled as she set aside the quilt. "That's because you come from a stable, loving home. You'll pass that along to your children someday."

Stephanie's smile was wistful. "I hope you're right."

ALEX CLICKED HIS CELL phone off and thought about the invitation Lissa had extended for Easter dinner. Daniel would have more fun going than having the two of them stay home. However, Alex; s pulse quickened at the thought that Stephanie would be there.. For someone who'd decided to back off, he was allowing himself to spend too much time with her.

People might get the wrong idea and begin to think of them as a couple. Would that be so bad? He imagined them walking through the park with Daniel between them.

He shook his head. He had to get rid of these thoughts. Stephanie hadn't been here long enough for him to truly know her. Though they'd spoken of their pasts, there might be things she hadn't yet disclosed. He could be setting himself up for disappointment if he didn't maintain an emotional boundary.

Each time he had this argument with himself, his resolve slipped further from his grasp. Though he might attribute it to Daniel's well-being, he would take Lissa up on her offer for Easter dinner because he, himself, wanted to go. Games, good food, and friends had finally become appealing again. He made his decision and called Lissa back.

"I'll take you up on that invitation. Tell me what to bring."

Lissa hesitated. "I don't know. Stephanie is bringing a veggie tray and pecan pie, and Grandma Mandy has everything else covered, except the fruit salad I'm doing. I was going to pick up some rolls, too."

"That's something I can do. I'll get them from The Bread Company. They make the best in the city. I'll bring along a couple of their spreads, too."

"That sounds delightful."

"We'll be there after church on Sunday," he promised.

When they hung up, Alex got his mind back on his work. A new client wanted an extensive garden make-over with wrought iron fencing and brick retaining walls. Alex had promised a rough design early the next week. It was going to take arduous work to meet the customer's request for completion by the end of May. He decided to get Stephanie's input tomorrow on the foliage, an area in which she had shown herself to be gifted.

Int the morning, he rapped on her doorframe, and she glanced up from her computer and greeted him. "You look like a drowning man. Do you need me to lend a hand?"

Running a hand through his hair, he said, "The workload is heavier than usual for this time of year. I have a pressing job now that needs completion by the end of May."

"How extensive is the work?"

He sighed. "Very. They're overhauling their entire backyard. That includes taking out a large patio, installing a fence, putting in a retaining wall on a slope, and working out a plan for summer vegetation. They want a central brick patio with a fireplace in the center."

"It sounds beautiful."

"It sounds like a lot of work."

She grinned. "That, too. We can make it happen. The mall job in Colorado is at a point where all I have to do is keep tabs on it."

"Okay. Then, I'd like you to search out bricks for the terrace in a blue tone to complement the patio. Also, we'll need ground cover for the summer. Could you come up with several possibilities for them to see?"

"Sure! I love big projects. I'll start on it tomorrow."

He smiled, knowing he wouldn't be disappointed. "I'll look forward to seeing your plans."

After an hour of work on the initial layout of the patio, he stopped for the day and picked up Daniel. They ate a favorite supper of macaroni and cheese. After stories and a bath, Daniel went down for the night.

As Alex sat in the living room looking over the work he'd forwarded to his laptop, doubts assailed him. It could be because he was fighting exhaustion, and the hour was getting late.

He'd come to depend on Stephanie for success with the higher volume of work they were getting. That was what he'd wanted. Yet if she became indispensable to him, it could be as Linda warned. Stephanie's departure for any reason would be a blow to the company and he would miss her more than he cared to admit.

He shut the computer, checked on Daniel, and got ready for bed. The house was chilly.

When he crawled beneath the covers, he was grateful for the warmth. Even so, sleep wouldn't come. Instead, he asked himself the tough questions. He'd allowed himself to be captivated by a dark-eyed beauty with a sunny smile. It was too late to deny his feelings. What he needed to determine was what to do about them.

When drowsiness eventually claimed him, he welcomed the reprieve. He would think more in the morning. Perhaps the way to proceed would be clearer then.

He awoke to hear Daniel crying. Half asleep, Alex scrambled out of bed. He reached his son to see him sitting up in bed. "Bugs, Daddy, bugs."

"Where?"

"In bed. See?" Daniel pointed to his covers.

Alex flipped on the night light. He checked the covers, scrutinizing them and finally shaking them. "I don't see anything, son. You had a bad dream."

Daniel clung to him. "Bugs, here."

He pointed to the shaken blanket.

Alex wasn't going to convince him. He scooped Daniel up. "You can spend the rest of the night with me. There are no bugs in my bed."

He hoped he wasn't starting something that would be hard to break. Still, Daniel needed comfort. Alex would worry later about forming a habit later.

They slept another three hours before the clock went off. By then, Daniel was sleeping soundly. It was difficult to get him awake. Daniel was still fussing when they drove to the sitter's house. The rough beginning left Alex unsettled when he got to work.

He called Stephanie into his office when she arrived. "Let's see what we can work up on the latest job."

"I started looking at bricks last night. I have some samples saved on my desktop."

Alex gestured to her office. "Let's go have a look."

He admired her dedication. She'd gone home and worked after hours to give them a head start on the new job. They worked well together, and the computer imaging was getting done in half the time it would take him by himself..

She pulled up a cream-colored brick wall, with a blue top layer of bricks. Right next to that image, she displayed the patio design with blue and beige squares. "What do you think of these?"

"They're a possibility. What else do you have?"

"I like this one." She showed him another with pink and blue-hued field stones, and then said, "I'll run through my slideshow of combinations I think would work. You can tell me what you think."

They spent the next hour shoulder-to-shoulder pouring over choices. They agreed on a half-dozen combinations to use in the plans they would show the clients.

"I'll take these combinations. You take those. We'll work out our designs and then tweak each other's work," he suggested.

She nodded. "Creativity is my favorite part of this job. I can't wait to play with all the choices and find something amazing."

Her enthusiasm was contagious. The fatigue that had plagued him on the way to work lifted. He worked, fueled by the pure joy of creation. He didn't stop until hunger gnawed in his stomach.

He went to the sitter, to check on Daniel and have lunch together. Then it was back to the office to see what Stephanie had accomplished.

"I came up with these three, but I like this best."

He studied the computer-designed plan and nodded. "I like it. I'm going to send my morning work over here and we'll compare."

He returned to his office. With a couple of quick clicks, she had copies of his plans.

They placed four of the designs simultaneously onto the screen. "I like your wall and my patio," he said. "Let's combine these into one picture and see how that looks."

Stephanie narrowed her gaze and studied the plans. "I like the combination of a stronger pink and blue rather than shades of gray."

"All right. Let's try the favorite mixture of what each of us likes."

When they'd played all the combinations, Stephanie liked her colors best. Alex felt slighted, though he knew it was ridiculous. She had no obligation to stroke his ego. He should be glad she was honest. He had asked for her opinion, so why did he feel unsettled by it?

They played with the programs for the rest of the afternoon until they each decided to draw up what they felt were the best designs, including what they would look like with spring foliage.

As they were leaving, Alex paused beside her door. "Daniel and I have been invited to Lissa and Jason's for Easter dinner next week. I understand you and Mandy will be there, too."

"Yes. I feel a little awkward since I'm not family. It won't feel so strange if you and Daniel are there."

"I'm glad. I hoped you wouldn't mind."

"The more the merrier at holidays. I used to wish my family were larger, with aunts and uncles and grandparents at dinner. It was always so quiet with just my parents and me."

Alex chuckled. "We went to our grandparents' house. All the cousins were there. There was always an egg hunt and a baseball game after a big dinner. Nothing about those dinners was quiet."

"But they were fun."

He nodded. "Yes, they were fun." As he left the office and drove home, he wished he could give Daniel the childhood he'd had. It was too still in their house with only two voices. He missed Kelly. She should be there with them. In time, there might have been other children. Eventually, they would have had the busy, happy house he craved. Now, it was too late. He couldn't bring Kelly back and he had not been able to move on with his life. He had not thought he wanted to until he met Stephanie.

CHAPTER SEVENTEEN

ON THE WAY HOME, STEPHANIE wondered why Alex would think she would object to having him with them on Easter. She was no more family to Lissa and Jason than he was.. They were being pitied, two people who needed company. Maybe someday she could return the favor to someone else who was alone.

Light rain slanted across the car window. She was glad it wasn't quite cold enough to freeze into ice on the streets. She hated ice and rarely had to deal with it in Georgia. It would be a relief to be snug and dry in Mandy's house.

Inside, she found a note on the kitchen table. Mandy explained she was at the hospital visiting the mother of a new baby. She'd left supper in the crockpot for them to be ready when she got back. Stephanie breathed deeply. The aroma of chicken stew made her stomach growl. She lifted the lid to see rich gravy, chunks of chicken, red pepper, and carrots. Fresh bread on the counter would complete their meal.

She decided to be useful and bring down the box of holiday decorations Mandy wanted from the attic. She'd mentioned going up for it and Stephanie had offered to do it for her. Mandy described where she would find the sealed box labeled 'seasonal decorations'. With Mandy's car gone, she had access to the pull-down ladder in the garage. Stephanie shivered as she yanked the cord and hauled down the stairs.

Carrying a flashlight, she climbed to the floored loft. A single light bulb with a twine pull cord lit the small drafty room. In the chill, Stephanie hurriedly scanned the boxes.

She felt relieved when she found the label she sought. Though the holiday decorations inside weren't heavy, the box was bulky. She balanced it carefully as she made her way back down the ladder from the now-black cavern above her.

On the last step, her foot slipped. With a cry of alarm, she fell backwards with the box. Her foot caught in the last rung of the ladder, and she sat down hard on the floor. The intense pain that shot through her ankle made her light-headed.

She managed to sit. There was no way she was going to stand. She needed someone with strong arms to support her to a car to drive her to the emergency room. One person came to mind. She fumbled in her pocket and got her cell phone, which miraculously survived the fall.

"Alex. I'm sorry to bother you at home. I slipped off a ladder in Mandy's garage and I think I've broken my ankle. Could you help me?"

"Of course. Where's Mandy? I'll have to be able to get into the garage."

"She's visiting a new mother at the hospital. I'll call her," she said, her voice shaky from the pain.

"Good. When she gets home, she can watch Daniel while I take you to the hospital."

"Okay, thanks."

She winced. Her ankle throbbed. She was relieved when Mandy answered her phone.

"Oh, my dear, I'll be right home! Don't try to move."

Mandy's tense tone relayed her worry.

Help was on the way. All Stephanie had to do was wait.

The minutes dragged by. Finally, the garage door ground upward on the hinges. Mandy rushed in holding Daniel while Alex strode forward and knelt beside her. "Let's see what it looks like."

Gently, he raised the hem of her pants and examined her ankle.

She held her leg straight out in front of her, not wanting to shift it. The throbbing was intense, and the swelling was obvious. Even with Alex's support, she imagined it was going to be hard to get up and stand on one leg.

"I left the car running and your door open," Alex said. "Let's get you inside."

He bent over. "Put your arm around my shoulder so I can help you up."

Mandy clucked her tongue. "You were getting the decorations for me. I'm so sorry you got hurt."

"It wasn't your fault," Stephanie assured her. "I wasn't as careful as I should have been."

Using only her good leg, she leaned hard against Alex's shoulder as he lifted her to stand on her good foot. She let out a gasp as the other one brushed the ground.

"This isn't worth the pain and effort," he said. He put one arm behind her back and the other under her knees and swept her off her feet into his arms.

Shocked by the intimacy, Stephanie protested. "I can stand and hobble if you'll help me."

"This is faster."

She clung to his neck, feeling the hard muscles of his chest. The familiarity of his aftershave gave her comfort. Though the situation was awkward, she couldn't deny the security she felt in his strong arms.

He settled her gently into the passenger seat, taking care not to bump her ankle.. He called to Mandy. "We'll be back in a little while."

She waved them off. "Don't worry. Daniel and I will be fine."

"I'm so sorry," Stephanie muttered as he put the car in gear. "I didn't know who else to call."

He glanced over at her. "It's perfectly all right. I'm glad I could help."

"I hope I haven't broken it. The thought of hobbling on crutches for weeks isn't appealing."

"Wait until you get it looked at before you worry."

She grimaced. "I'm not good at that."

They turned left off of Main Street onto the side road to the hospital. Her ankle throbbed continuously, and the pain was more intense. She berated herself for losing her balance. If she'd been more careful she wouldn't be sitting here in agony taking up Mandy's and Alex's time.

Darkness had fallen when Alex stopped in front of the emergency room's sliding glass doors. "I'm going in for a wheelchair."

He raised a brow and added, "Unless you want me to carry you inside."

The idea was embarrassing. "No, please. The wheelchair will be fine."

He nodded and opened the door to get out. A chilly breeze entered the car. She hadn't thought to ask for her coat when they left the house. Alex would give her his suede coat if she asked. She wasn't about to do so. She'd put him out enough already.

She watched him walk through the entrance, hoping he would return fast. A few minutes passed and a young woman pushing a wheelchair followed him quickly to the car. Alex opened Stephanie's door and took her arm. He helped her onto her good foot and pivoted her as the blond woman, whose name tag read, "Paula," steadied the wheelchair behind her.

Stephanie sat down, relief washing over her, knowing her ankle would be taken care of.

When the footrest was raised, Stephanie stifled a cry of pain as Paula gently settled her ankle in position. As she was rolled toward the doors, she heard the wail of an ambulance in the distance.

Once that person was inside, Stephanie knew that there would be someone who needed help more desperately than she did.. The realization snuffed out the self-pity that had crept into her mind.

She registered at the desk as the paramedics wheeled the patient in and rushed through the ER doors. A count of the other patients gave her a mental calculation of how long she would wait. At least eight people were ahead of her. It could be a couple of hours. Maybe longer.

The television mounted on the wall played a modern sitcom with clever children exchanging one-liners with each other. Growing bored, she fidgeted with her birthstone ring. Instead of a real diamond for April, it was an affordable cubic zirconium her parents had bought her when she turned fourteen.

"Would you like a magazine?" Alex asked.

She shook her head. "No thanks. I don't think I could concentrate."

"It hurts a lot?"

"It throbs but I know there are people here in a lot more pain than I am."

"I admire your attitude. I have a hard time thinking that way when I'm the one hurting."

"Me, too, actually. It didn't occur to me until I heard that ambulance arriving and then I thought of all the frightening emergencies they tend to," she said.

A couple of hours later, a nurse called her name and Alex wheeled her to the door.

"We're going to take your information and vitals. It shouldn't be too much longer until we have a room."

Alex left her with the nurse. Though Stephanie knew there might be personal questions to answer, she missed his calming presence. In a short time, she'd come to trust him and wished they shared more than a business acquaintance.

She focused on the nurse's questions and not the loneliness she felt. A short while later, she was wheeled back to the waiting room. Alex glanced up and pushed a chair out of the way next to where he was sitting.

"How are you doing? Is the pain worse?" he asked.

"It's about the same. I wouldn't want to have to walk on that foot," she said.

A glance at her watch showed they'd been waiting for approximately four hours. "Have you checked on Daniel?" she asked.

He nodded. "I called while you were with the nurse. Mandy said he was fine and. he was asleep on the couch. She told me that earlier, when they were coloring, she thinks he was drawing flowers and trees."

"Maybe he's been hacking into your landscape files."

He touched his chin in a thoughtful gesture. "Maybe I should rename my company Lance and Son Landscapers."

Nodding, she answered, "I wouldn't be surprised if he has as good of an eye for layout and colors as his dad does. Someday, he might join you."

Alex warmed at her compliment.

Becoming more serious, Alex said, "Maybe. However, I decided when he was born, that I would encourage him to pursue his own interests. It's more important to enjoy a job than it is to please a father. I was always glad my parents didn't pressure me into a certain profession. I had friends who faced constant criticism for their choices of occupations."

"I was blessed with supportive parents, also. I used their yard for my playground of botany projects. They never knew what was going to be coming up next."

"I bet they didn't mind," Alex said.

"I suppose not. They seem to like my ideas for their new property in Florida."

"That's the payoff for your early experiments."

Stephanie was grateful for the conversation that provided a diversion from the pain of her ankle, "I was always planting things in odd places. One year I asked a neighbor for a sprig from her peppermint plant. I put it in my mother's front flower bed, and it took over. I remember the work we did to weed it all out until it stopped coming up."

"Maybe you could have turned it into an herbal tea business," he suggested.

"My mother would rather have had her mums."

Finally, a nurse called her name Alex wheeled her forward and then gave her care over to the dark-haired, middle-aged woman who took her to a room.

The room where she was brought was well-lit and tiny. Machines lay along the far wall on the other side of a narrow bed. "Let's have you stay in the wheelchair until the doctor comes in. She may want to send you right out for an X-ray."

Stephanie was happy enough to stay put. The thought of hopping to the bed made her cringe. The nurse hooked her up to a machine that took her pulse and blood pressure while the nurse took her temperature. The nurse then left her alone to wait. Stephanie wished Alex was with her.

The doctor arrived and gave her a reassuring smile. "You hurt your ankle? How did it happen?"

"I slipped off of a ladder."

"Let's take a look."

She fingered her ankle carefully. Touching select spots, she asked, "Does this hurt?"

Stephanie winced as the doctor examined a tender spot. "It's very sore there," Stephanie said.

"I'm going to send you to X-ray to make sure there's no break. Then we'll decide on the treatment. Someone will be right in to get you."

She waited again and a cheery aide came to wheel her to have her X-ray. "They're ready for you. I'll try to give you a smooth ride."

They went down two long halls, turning right and then left. The aide parked her in the waiting room. A technician stepped out. "Thanks, Libby," he told the aide. "We'll take it from here."

Fortyish and balding, he made small talk as he set her up for the x-ray. Her ankle throbbed unbearably as he manipulated her leg into position. Stepping from the room, he clicked the pictures.

He came back and smiled reassuringly. "We'll get these read by the doc and get you fixed up. I'll call someone to take you back to the ER."

Apparently, Libby was busy. An efficient, but less talkative woman pushed her back. It wasn't long until the doctor returned. "The good news is there's not a break. You have a bad sprain with a good deal of swelling. We're going to wrap it and prescribe an anti-inflammatory. You'll need to stay off that ankle for a couple of weeks. Your regular doctor can follow up."

"I'm pretty new in town. I don't have a doctor yet."

"You can check with our outpatient office to see who's taking new patients. After you make an appointment, let us know where to send the X-ray."

"All right. I guess this means crutches. Where do I get them?"

"You can buy them in most stores that have a pharmacy or rent them from one in the medical center on 30th Street."

"Okay. Thanks."

After he left, a nurse entered, handed her a prescription, and bound her ankle. "Keep the wrapping on and avoid putting full weight on this foot," she advised.

Stephanie grimaced. "The pain will remind me. I want to know how to take a shower with the elastic binding on."

The nurse said," Wrap it in a garbage bag, secure the top with duct tape. Then, take a second garbage bag and secure it above the first one. With care, there should be no water that gets inside."

The slight jostling required to wrap it had been painfully uncomfortable. With Easter coming next week, she needed the injury to heal quickly, or she wasn't going to be much help cooking Mandy's Easter dinner.

Alex stood to meet her as yet another aide wheeled her back to the waiting room. His expectant expression showed he was waiting for an update. "Is it broken?"

"No. It's just a bad sprain. I have to get crutches. The doctor said stores with pharmacies have them."

After wheeling her to the car, Alex and the aide helped her into the front seat. When they were both inside, Alex said, "Before you buy crutches, let me talk to Linda. She sprained her foot about a year ago and hobbled around on some. She may still have them."

Stephanie bit her lip. "I don't think I'm her favorite person."

She noted his raised eyebrow.

"What makes you say that?"

She felt her cheeks grow warm. She didn't want to explain it to him, but the words slipped out of her mouth. "She doesn't trust me. She thinks I want to take over the business."

"Really? How would you do that?"

Stephanie squirmed in her seat. "First, I sweep you off your feet. Then, when you're madly in love, I marry you and tell you how to run your company."

Alex pursed his lips. "That wouldn't be your style."

Surprised, she turned to face him. "How do you think I'd steal your company?"

"You wouldn't deceive me. You'd simply become invaluable to me. If I couldn't afford to lose you, I'd have to do whatever you said."

"I don't come out nice either way."

"But, you see, I don't believe either scenario."

"Are you sure?"

He hesitated for only a second. "I'm sure."

His delay told her all she needed to know. He didn't totally trust her. Her enthusiasm and talent had made her suspect. How long would it take for them to believe she had no hidden agenda?

"Don't bother Linda. She's probably busy. Mandy can help me get the crutches."

He frowned.

She wondered if he knew she felt hurt.

His jaw tightened. "That doesn't make sense. No one's using them."

"No. You've been a tremendous help tonight. I don't want to impose on Linda. I want to go back to Mandy's house."

"All right."

They both grew quiet.

When they reached Mandy's house, Stephanie opened her door to get out.. As she put her good foot on the ground, Alex came around to help her out of the car.

"Let me help you," Alex said.

She leaned against him as he supported her to the front door. The light spilling from the windows was warm and welcoming. She couldn't wait to get out of the darkness and put her aching ankle up on the couch in the warm parlor.

Mandy appeared, holding Daniel in her arms.

Alex helped Stephanie to the sofa and then turned to take Daniel. "Thank you for watching him."

"You were helping my roommate."

She turned to Stephanie. "How are you, dear?"

"It's a bad sprain. I'm supposed to keep it wrapped and elevated. I need a prescription filled and I need to find a doctor."

"And she needs crutches," Alex said.

Mandy turned and strode toward the entryway closet. "I have an old pair in here from when my son twisted his knee. They should work for you, Stephanie."

"You're in good hands now. I'll take Daniel home to bed."

Stephanie sighed. No matter what he thought of her, Alex had come to her rescue. She owed him a debt of gratitude.

She looked him squarely in the eyes and tried to ignore the impact of his blue gaze. "You went out of your way for me. Thank you."

"You're welcome."

The searching look in his eyes haunted her for the rest of the evening.

.

CHAPTER EIGHTEEN

MANDY FUSSED OVER HER as she stacked couch pillows for Stephanie to raise her ankle. "Does it hurt a lot?"

Touched by her motherly concern, Stephanie answered. "Not too much if I keep it still. I have a prescription for an anti-inflammatory that I need to fill."

In keeping with her nature, Mandy said, "You give it to me, and I'll run to do it right now."

"Thanks. I don't know what I'd do without you."

Mandy huffed. "You wouldn't have sprained your ankle."

"You never know. I might have tripped somewhere else."

"Nonetheless, I owe you for this one. When I get back from the pharmacy, I'll bring you a nice plate of food. Now you just rest a bit."

Mandy took the script, got her purse, and hurried out. Alone in the house, Stephanie pondered her reaction to Alex and his possible lack of trust. Why did it bother her so much?

The answer seemed obvious. She cared about the man much more than she should. Wanting his business to grow had nothing to do with her gain. She wanted Alex to be happy and reap rewards from both of their hard work. To that end, she'd been happy to put in long hours. All she asked in return was his trust. If she couldn't gain that, it was only a matter of time until she had to leave the company.

She was surprised t she dozed off when Mandy returned and awakened her. A draft of chilly air followed Mandy inside as she bustled through the parlor. "I'm getting you some food to take with your medicine. We don't want it to upset your stomach."

She'd had an early lunch hours ago and the mention of food made her stomach rumble.

Mandy handed her a plate. "I ate a bite with Daniel, but here's yours. I reheated it for you."

The stew smelled tantalizing. She took her medicine and dug in and found it tasted as good as it smelled. A buttered slice of homemade bread on the side completed her dinner.

They chatted while she ate. Mandy showed her decorations from the box Stephanie was holding when she fell. Pinecone turkeys made by her son when he was a child, an autumn wreath crafted by Mandy, and silk flower arrangements in fall colors had been carefully packed inside.

Mandy showed Stephanie rust-colored linen napkins with brass holders. "These have been in my family for quite a while. I use them on the Thanksgiving table each year along with this tablecloth."

She pulled a linen cloth out of the box, bearing fall leaves and a bottom border of pumpkins and cornucopias.

Stephanie sucked in a breath. "That's beautiful. I didn't grow up with a tradition of decorating for holidays. On Thanksgiving, we always went out to eat. When my friends complained about leftovers, I envied them. I thought it would be nice to have turkey and pie for a few more days."

Mandy chuckled. "You'll get your wish this year. I probably won't cook except with the leftovers for almost a week."

"Good. I'm looking forward to it," Stephanie stated. She'd finally get her fill of a holiday that didn't seem to slip by too quickly.

From the bottom of the box, Mandy pulled out a bag with plastic Easter eggs, a wind-up fluffy yellow chick that walked and peeped, and a plush Easter bunny that patted his foot to the Easter parade song.

"These are cute," Stephanie said.

"I thought we'd take them to Lissa's house. Alex is bringing Daniel. He'll like to hunt the eggs and play with the toys."

"He probably wasn't old enough last year to hunt eggs," Stephanie said.

"No, but he'll be fun this year."

When Stephanie finished eating a bowl of cobbler, Mandy showed her how to use the crutches. It took some adjusting and practicing before she felt steady on them. "I don't have enough coordination for these."

"Once you use them for a day or two, you'll be an expert," Mandy assured her.

They chatted for a few more minutes and Mandy watched Stephanie use the crutches as she went down the ahl to go to bed.. sore.

The next morning Stephanie awoke to find her ankle still swollen and sore. Hobbling carefully along on the crutches, she made her way to the kitchen. Mandy had brewed fragrant almond-scented coffee.. She set Stephanie's rose mug on the table along with a plate of bacon and toast.

"What a wonderful breakfast for a chilly morning," Stephanie declared.

"You'll need extra energy to manage on crutches. Would you like me to give you a ride to work?"

"Thanks, but I can manage since I hurt my left ankle instead of my right."

"If you're sure I certainly don't mind helping you out. At least let me pack your lunch. I have ham and Swiss or egg salad for sandwiches. Which would you like?"

"Egg salad, please. It's kind of you."

"No trouble, dear. After all, you did secure my decorations at the expense of your ankle."

"It will heal. I plan to help you with Easter dinner preparations on Saturday night."

"There is plenty you can do to help while sitting down, measuring and stirring, for example."

"I'll be happy to do whatever you need."

Mandy put lunch together while Stephanie finished getting ready for work. Mandy accompanied her to the car and made sure she was settled before handing her the brown bag packed with delectable food. She waved goodbye to Mandy, started the car, and drove down the street.

Her conversation with Alex the previous evening still haunted her. She wondered if his hesitation regarding her aspirations would make things awkward between them today. It seemed the only way she could make things right was to do her job in a robot-like way with no fresh ideas of how to improve his business. If that were what he wanted, he would have to find someone else to do it.

She arrived with her emotions in high gear, feeling it was unfair to be judged ambitious when all she wanted to do was to help. Nonetheless, as long as he employed her, she would further his business in every way she could.

She managed to stand on her good foot and retrieve the crutches from the backseat. As she walked through the reception area, she was relieved that Linda was not yet at her desk.

. Once settled in her office, she checked email-for an update on the job underway in Colorado. Fortunately, it was proceeding on schedule.

A few moments later, Linda appeared in her doorway. "I had some errands to run this morning before I came to work. Alex told me about your ankle injury. I was sorry to hear about it. Is it terribly painful?"

"It's not too bad. I have some pills to help with the pain."

"I hope it gets better fast/ Let me know if you need anything."

Stephanie thanked Linda for her concern and Linda returned to the reception area.

When Alex popped in, he asked about her ankle and how she was feeling. "If it gets too sore, it's fine for you to go home and rest," he said.

"It feels all right now. I took a pain pill this morning."

"I'm glad for that. I'd like your input on the changes he'd made to their joint design.

"The rough-hewn rocks surrounding the waterfall on the slope are a nice touch. Have you thought about putting one on the other side?

They would be in balance on either side of the brick stairs going down," she said.

He nodded. "That's a good suggestion. Let me grab my laptop and we'll look at it together.

Returning, he typed into the program, and copied the image of the waterfall to the other side. He studied it for a moment. "I see what you mean. It completes the circle around the fire pit at the center of the bottom patio."

"You took out the rose bushes along the back fence and put in the hedge instead, "she said.

"I did. I liked the look of it better."

Stephanie held her tongue, though she didn't agree. The roses had been her idea.

Normally, the change wouldn't have bothered her. She was being overly sensitive, no doubt, and feeling unappreciated. She reminded herself she was to work not to please man but to please the Lord. A measure of peace settled over her at the thought. Why did she care what others thought of her if her conscience was clear with God?

They discussed the design for a few more moments before Alex returned to his office. She concentrated on the job at hand for the rest of the morning. At noon, she took out the egg salad sandwich Mandy had packed.

Alongside it, she discovered potato chips, an apple, and two chocolate chip cookies. She set them on her desk with anticipation. A long morning of work had claimed her attention, as did her ankle. She hadn't realized she had grown hungry.

A moment later, Alex rapped on her doorframe. She glanced up. He cocked his head, a sympathetic expression on his face. "I guess you're eating in today. How's your ankle feeling now?"

"It still hurts but the medicine is helping.. The swelling has gone down a little."

"Is there anything I can get you or do for you before I go to eat with Daniel?"

"No. Thank you. I have a lunch lovingly packed by Mandy."

"I envy you. My lunch was hurriedly packed by me."

"I don't believe I'll offer to trade with you," she quipped.

"I don't blame you. I hope you're still coming to Easter dinner."

She nodded. "I'm still helping Mandy cook. She's giving me work I can do sitting down."

"I'm glad your hurt ankle didn't change your plans. Will you be going to church on Sunday?"

"Yes. Hopefully, my arms and arm pits won't be as sore from managing the crutches by then. Since there aren't any stairs in the church hallway, I shouldn't have too much trouble."

"There are a few stairs going into the building. Luckily, there's a ramp leading in from the side. Why don't you let me come by for you and Mandy? Then I could help you navigate into the church.."

Did he feel sorry for her hobbling around clumsily on her sticks? "You're kind. I think it will work.

He didn't hesitate. "I don't mind going to class this week. Hopefully, Daniel will stay well. I'll come by at eight-thirty for both or you."

Without another word, he turned from the doorway, and she heard his footsteps padding away down the hall. She tried to discern his offer. Did he think of her as a burden? The idea roused her independent nature.

NONETHELESS, MANDY was pleased by his offer, and they were ready promptly at eight-thirty on Easter morning. Alex helped them into coats before accompanying them into a bright morning.

As they drove down the block, Stephanie was struck by ornamental cherry trees thrusting pink-blossomed branches toward an azure sky. Though she'd slept poorly, trying to get comfortable with her sore ankle, the bright sunshine raised her spirits.

Mandy had insisted upon sitting in the back next to Daniel in his car seat.

"You'll have more room to get out without bumping your leg," she told Stephanie.

Stephanie glanced at Alex as he drove toward the church. She wished his profile didn't appeal to her more than any man she'd ever met. If she didn't get control over the errant feelings that increasingly swept over her, she would eventually have to change jobs. It would become torture to work beside him each day and pretend he wasn't the most handsome man she'd ever met.

Would he believe the truth of her feelings? She didn't throw herself into work due to a desire to take control of his company. She just wanted him to be happy and successful.

As they parked in the lot closest to the church, Mandy leaned forward to say, "After Sunday school, some of us are taking filled Easter eggs to a park for an egg hunt for disadvantaged children. I can get a ride back with one of the ladies Do you think you could take Stephanie home?" Mandy asked Alex.

"I can go along with you, Mandy. I don't mind," Stephanie said.

"I'm more than happy to give you a ride back," Alex offered.

"Good. It might be a little crowded with all the bags of eggs," Mandy said.

Cheeks burning, Stephanie hoped Alex didn't think she had anything to do with suddenly springing this on him.

"While I'm at your house, I can pick up any food or other things that are going to Lissa and Jason's house. Stephanie can tell me what goes. Then you won't have to worry about it when you get back," Alex told Mandy.

"That's a good idea. I got up extra early and snuck out to go to Lissa's house and start the ham. All that's left to bring later is just a bit more food and Easter goodies. Are you sure you can manage to load them with Daniel in tow?"

Alex chuckled. "He likes to help now. If I give him something small to carry, he'll think it's great fun."

"Wonderful. Don't let him peek in the sack. I want it to be a surprise," Mandy said. "And don't let Stephanie hobble around the house doing things. She should rest her ankle until I get back."

Alex grinned as he opened Stephanie's door and helped her onto her crutches. "I'll threaten to take credit for one of her designs if she moves from the couch."

"You won't know what I do once you leave," she taunted back.

"Are you asking me to stay to keep an eye on you?"

Her cheeks warmed at the direction of the conversation. "No. I can be trusted to take care of myself."

Alex shook his head. "I don't know."

Mandy got Daniel out of his seat and joined them. "Let's go worship up an appetite," she said.

After dropping Daniel in the nursery, Alex joined them in the church that was filled with Easter lilies in full bloom. The sweet scent of the flowers filled the church. A tall brass pedestal held the white Easter candle and a hand-woven wall hanging of the empty tomb graced one side of the altar.

The sermon seemed expressly written for Stephanie. She listened closely to the admonition to leave the future to God. The pastor assured his flock that God had a plan for their lives, just as He'd had a plan for His Son All they needed to do was listen and follow, one day at a time.

Stephanie felt a smile curve her lips. She'd been so concerned about her job and the fear that she'd be forced to find another, that she'd let stress take over her life. She no longer felt this worry. She was determined to trust and not to worry. No matter what happened, her future was firmly in God's hands.

The tension that suddenly lifted from her shoulders and neck was replaced by a sense of freedom and adventure. She would do her best to ensure everyone had a nice time together today. Her heart was light, though her crutches slowed her progress down as Alex and she walked down the corridor to the classroom.

Though two members had brought guests, the attendance was down due to the holiday. Many of the members had skipped class to prepare for their Easter dinners with their families.

Alex made a beeline for the donuts. Stephanie called after him. "What about the appetite you've worked up? Isn't this going to dampen it?"

He scooped up a red, frosted donut with sprinkles. Grinning at her, he set it on a napkin. "Nope. Can I get one for you?"

"No thanks. I'll wait for Easter dinner."

She plopped into a chair, feeling ungainly as she set the crutches beside her. One of the regular attendees approached, perching on the chair beside her. "What happened?"

After Stephanie relayed the story of the fall, the pretty blond, Patti, gave her a pitying look. "It's sad you'll be on crutches today on Easter!. You're lucky to be with Mandy. Some people in your shoes would miss a good Easter dinner. You don't have to worry about that."

"No, I don't." Despite her inconvenience, her heart swelled with gratitude that God had placed her with a kindly woman who fussed over her. She was truly blessed.

When the class ended, she held back until the hall cleared. "You get Daniel. I'll wait for you in the foyer. That way, I won't create a traffic jam."

"Sounds good. I'll be right back."

When he returned with Daniel, the child held his arms out to her.

"Stephanie can't hold you right now. She hurt her ankle," Alex said.

They proceeded slowly to the car. All the while, Daniel puzzled over what had happened to Stephanie. A worried frown creased his tiny forehead as he asked, "Leg broke?"

Stephanie clunked along on the crutches. "It's not broken, honey. I hurt my ankle and can't stand on it. It will get better."

Daniel pointed to a scratch on his arm. "I hurt arm."

Stephanie smiled at the child. "I see you did. How did you hurt it?"

"Daddy hammer it. Bang," he replied.

Stephanie raised a brow at Alex, who flushed becomingly.

"He scratched his arm on a nail head that was sticking out in his closet. I hammered it back in."

Stephanie stifled her amusement. "I'm sorry you hurt your arm," she told Daniel.

His conversational skills were growing. He was changing rapidly from a baby to a little boy. Stephanie found the process as fascinating as an orchid coming into bloom. She had no doubt he was a bright child who would always keep Alex on his toes.

She gave Alex the key to unlock the front door and they went inside. She then led them to the kitchen where the food waited to be transported. Stephanie had made two pies and Mandy was providing a whipped topping.

Leaning on one crutch, she opened the refrigerator. "The potato salad and relish tray are in here. So is the whipped topping. My pies are on the counter. Mandy made a fruit salad that's in this bowl."

She pointed to a ceramic bowl with a clear cover. "Are you going to be able to get all this stuff there without any of it spilling? I know Mandy has a couple of boxes in the garage. Would that help?"

"I think it would," he replied. "You and Daniel go sit in the living room and solve the problems of the world while I get the boxes and load the food. Then you can check to be sure I got everything," Alex said.

Stephanie was more than ready to get off her good foot. "Come on honey. I'll tell you a story while Daddy works."

Daniel followed her into the living room. She told him a story she made up about a happy dragon that had a dog for a pet. He listened raptly until the dragon and dog lived happily ever after in the dragon's cave with lots of balls to chase and lots of bones to chew.

When Alex finished loading the boxes into the car, he came into the living room and said,. "Do you want to check in the kitchen to make sure I get everything?"

She entered the kitchen and did a mental check and didn't see anything he'd missed. Even if he did, she and Mandy could bring it over later. One thing was for sure. They were going to have an amazing Easter meal.

"It looks like you have it all," she said.

Alex squatted beside Daniel and hugged him. "Did you and Stephanie solve the problems of the world?"

Daniel cocked his head to look at his daddy.

Stephanie answered for him. "Yes, we did. If everyone had a puppy and all the ice cream they wanted, we'd have no more wars."

"That sounds like advice from a two-year-old. I think it just might work," Alex said. He held Daniel in his arms as Stephanie escorted them into the foyer.to tell them good-bye.

"Rest up. I plan on being a busy bunny when I get to Lissa's house. Remember, I might need a pair of keen eyes to help me remember where I hide some of the eggs," he said.

"I don't think you'll be hiding them too hard for a two-year-old," she replied.

"I'm creative, like you." The tenderness of his smile made her heart flip.

She had to stop letting him affect her so deeply. He certainly didn't try to make her feel like a lovesick schoolgirl. She managed that entirely on her own.

She spent the time until Mandy returned struggling to keep her mind off her handsome boss. It was hard enough to ignore the attraction while working with him. Easter was a social time, with no business interactions to act as a buffer. She would have to guard her heart.

CHAPTER NINETEEN

WHEN MANDY RETURNED, Stephanie said, "Someone raided your refrigerator while you were gone."

Mandy smiled in return. "What a sweet man to help us out like that."

Stephanie wasn't sure how to answer without having Mandy read too much into what she said. Finally, she answered, "That was very considerate. Did you get all your eggs delivered?"

"Yes. When I left, the volunteers were hiding them in the park."

Mandy checked the refrigerator and assured Stephanie that Alex had found all the food for Easter dinner. All that was left was for the two women to drive over to Lissa's house.

"How's your ankle feeling?" Mandy asked when they were on their way.

"It aches when I move it, but not so much when I hold still."

"Then we'll see that you hold still once we get there."

When they arrived, Jason greeted them at the front door and ushered them into the living room. Resurrection hymns were playing softly in the background. The table held a container of Easter lilies with a silver cross embossed on the shiny gold foil that covered the vase.

"What a beautiful plant," Stephanie told Jason. "Where did you get it?"

"I got it for Lissa. The beauty of it being a live plant is that I can plant it outside in May."

"You'll enjoy it for a long time," Stephanie said. "I hear it's not safe to plant until after Mother's Day in this climate."

"That's true. We could have a freeze until then. Now and then we even get zapped with a freeze after Mother's Day."

Stephanie chuckled. "I'm not in Georgia anymore."

Alex arrived with Daniel and the rolls. He set them on the counter that separated the two rooms. "You look like you've been busy," he told Lissa.

"I've had lots of help." She motioned to the kitchen. "Stephanie made the pies and Mandy did the rest."

Jason objected. "What about me? I've been slaving away making iced tea and tasting ham to be sure it's done."

"I thought that would be my job," Alex said.

Raising his eyebrows, Jason shook his head. "I'm not sure there's much left."

"Despite his efforts, there's plenty," Mandy assured them, stepping back from the stove.

Alex held Daniel up. "Good. I've brought a hungry man."

Though he was pleased to see all of them, Alex's gaze drifted through the kitchen until he spotted who he'd been truly seeking. Stephanie was now sitting at the small dinette table.

"Let's take a tour of the kitchen," Alex told Daniel.

"It's a minefield in here. You can't get out without being a guinea pig," Jason said.

Alex's eyes met Stephanie's gaze. "Treacherous, huh? We'll brave it."

He carted Daniel around the room.

Mandy turned with a smile. "Don't you both look handsome? Everything's almost done. If you're hungry, you can grab some veggies and dip while you wait."

"You hear that, Daniel? You can have a carrot stick and dip. Does that sound good?" Alex asked.

Daniel nodded.

The dip tray was at the table where Stephanie worked on a punch made with orange sherbet, and lemon-lime soda to go with dessert.

"You can taste this if you'll set it on the counter for me," she offered. Her glossy dark hair swung at her shoulders as she cocked her head to speak to him.

Setting Daniel on the floor with his carrot stick, Alex said, "Sure. I'd be glad to help. How's your ankle feeing now?"

"Still achy, but better each day. I've been keeping it propped up at night. I think that's helping.

"That's good. I'm sure Mandy didn't let you overdo working on the meal."

"No. She kept me chained to the table yesterday. I sliced, diced, measured, and mixed."

"I hope you copied all her recipes. You could make a mint selling them."

"Nope. She kept me too busy."

He carried the punch bowl to the counter and arranged the cut crystal cups around the matching bowl. The festive spirit in the house raised Alex's spirits from the loneliness he'd struggled with earlier in the day.

Everyone worked to set the dishes of food along the counter. Alex found the mingling aromas tantalizing. His stomach rumbled. They gathered in front of their plates in the living room for Jason to say the Easter blessing. Alex held Daniel in his arms, pleased when the child folded his tiny hands for the prayer.

When they finished, they congregated along the serving bar to spoon potato salad rich with egg and mayonnaise, fruit salad with berries and pineapple, buttery rolls, and vegetables and dip. The ham sat carved in tender slices next to the dish of chunky potato salad.

Lissa chuckled. "I believe I have more on my plate than I'll be able to eat."

She rubbed her rounded stomach.

"Not I," Alex said. "I'll eat and enjoy every mouthful."

"Better save room for my pie," Stephanie said.

"We'll all save room for dessert," Jason added. "It's the best part of any meal."

They settled at the table with Daniel in Alex's lap. They shared dinner, and when Daniel finished he scampered down to play with the wind-up chick and singing bunny Mandy had brought.

Alex was relieved to have him amused for a while. Alex could enjoy adult conversation, and more especially, Stephanie's company. She looked beautiful. Her soft features were accented by ringlets that had formed along her forehead, and her animated expression made him feel more alive than he had in two years.

She nodded to him as she answered Lissa's question regarding sightseeing near her new home.

"I haven't been anywhere farther than Durango, Colorado. My boss keeps me too busy to see the acclaimed scenery of the southwest."

"I remember a certain lady who arranged sightseeing for me and Lissa. Look where that led," Jason said.

Mandy gave him a knowing smile. "For that, you'll be forever grateful."

"So true," he said. "As soon as I met Lissa, I knew she was who I wanted to marry. It took a little longer to convince her that she wanted me."

"I was playing hard to get," Lissa replied, giving him a coy look from across the table.

"You couldn't resist my charm," Jason said.

He turned to Alex. "I had to make up enough excuses to spend time with her to convince her to marry me."

Alex nodded. Inwardly, he wondered if that was what he'd been doing. Were picnics, taking Stephanie to lunch, and going back to Sunday school were his ways to be close to her? Whether he liked it or not, it was her face he looked forward to seeing when he got to work each morning.

"We should have dessert," Mandy stated. "I saved just enough room for a piece of Stephanie's pecan pie."

"I hope it turned out all right. It's been a long time since I've baked anything."

"It was your grandmother's recipe. We'll taste a bit of history," Mandy stated.

Alex claimed a generous slice of pecan pie to share with Daniel. In truth, his son would eat little, and Alex was looking forward to trying Stephanie's contribution.

They piled thick dollops of whipped topping atop their desserts and carried them to the table. Daniel ate two bites before slipping back to play. After the first bite of Stephanie's dessert, Alex was hooked. "This is good. Your grandmother must have been an amazing cook."

"It's wonderful," the others echoed.

Stephanie smiled as a charming flush crept across her cheeks. "Thank you. My grandma was a good baker. She helped us with bake sales as a kid."

When everyone had sampled all they could hold, everyone except Stephanie and Daniel pitched in to carry the dishes into the kitchen. Since they were soon stepping in each other's way, Mandy sent Lissa and Jason out. "You hosted us. It won't take long to put up the food and load the dishes."

"We'll hide eggs while Stephanie watches," Lissa said.

"How about playing a dictionary word game after Daniel's egg hunt?" Jason asked.

"Sure," Alex answered. "I was hoping for a game of croquet like Stephanie described in her celebrations as a kid. I don't suppose you have a croquet set."

"I'm afraid we don't," Jason said.

"That's a nice tradition," Lissa told Stephanie. "Those are the things that keep families close. Jason and I want to have special holiday customs with our little one."

Alex sighed. "I should do more with Daniel. When it's just the two of us, I get lazy and take the easy way out. The poor guy would have had a take-out meal for dinner if not for your kindness."

When Alex and Mandy finished cleaning the kitchen, everyone gathered on the patio to watch Daniel hunt plastic eggs. Mandy handed him a small green basket and Alex showed Daniel one of the eggs and explained that Daniel should find the others. There were ten in all that Mandy had filled with stickers and other small goodies. Once Daniel understood, it didn't take him long to cover the patio and scoop up the eggs.

Back inside the house, Daniel was content to open the eggs and explore the prizes, while the grown-ups began the dictionary game. Instead of playing, Mandy insisted on sitting with Daniel. By the end of the last round, Daniel grew drowsy as Mandy rocked him.

When the team of Lissa and Jason won, Alex decided it was time to take his sleepy son home. He turned to his hosts. "I suppose I should get Daniel down for his nap. Thank you for including us. It's been a wonderful day. "

"We enjoyed having you," Lissa assured him.

Mandy helped Alex get Daniel bundled into his jacket. "He'll fall asleep on the way home," she predicted.

"He probably will," Alex agreed.

He turned to Stephanie. "Don't think about work today. Give yourself Easter Day off."

"I'll try. Still, sometimes ideas pop into my head."

"Yes. That happens to me, too. But that's okay for me. It's my company. You deserve the day off."

Her lips parted slightly as though she would comment and then they closed. He decided she'd understood his message. The risk and responsibility for this business were his alone. He was the boss.

The lonely feeling returned as he drove home with Daniel fast asleep. It would be fun to have someone to talk to for the rest of the afternoon and evening. He considered turning on the television for the comforting sound of voices. However, the impersonal nature of television made him depressed.

He settled on the sofa to look at the newspaper after putting Daniel down for his nap. There were days he didn't get around to reading it at all. Today, it was filled with ads for garden products. The garden stores would be busy from now until the beginning of fall.

He wondered what Stephanie was doing. Was she thinking about him? He shut the thought out of his mind. He had no reason to believe she felt any romantic interest. It was better to keep his mind on his job.

AFTER THE FOLLOWING busy week of work, Stephanie slept soundly on Saturday morning until her alarm woke her. She was surprised to see the sun already shining brightly through the lacy curtains. She wrapped herself in her robe and then headed to the kitchen in the hopes of finding hot coffee.

Mandy hadn't disappointed her. The pot simmered and the aroma drew her. She poured a generous mug and helped herself to a blueberry muffin from a plateful that Mandy had left on the table.

The house lay quiet. Where was Mandy? She wasn't usually out this early.

When Stephanie finished, she loaded her dishes into the dishwasher. She planned to wipe the counters, yet the kitchen was already spotless. The chrome sink shone, and the counters were wiped.

She wasn't sure what to do. Mandy had kindly done her laundry, and for the first time, she wished she were at work instead of enjoying the luxury of time off. In reality, honesty compelled her to admit it wasn't her work she missed. It was Alex.

She felt more alive when they were together than she ever had on her own. With their heads bent over a project, they seemed like one entity. She'd never felt that way with any other man.

It pained her to know his heart was still tied to Kelly. Though his loyalty was romantic, it was not directed at her. So, she would keep her secret. He would never know how much she'd come to care for him.

She settled on the sofa with a mystery novel. However, after reading the same page three times, she sighed in exasperation and set the book aside. Perhaps work would take her mind off Alex.

She flipped her laptop open and connected with her computer in the office to access her files. The vegetation and water features along the slope still needed refining. Soon, she was immersed in various colors of plants and rocks to form the miniature waterfalls.

When Mandy came in at noon carrying an armload of fabric, Stephanie was surprised that the last two hours had flown by so quickly. A smile creased the corners of her mouth. The material that Mandy carried was brightly patterned with teddy bears and kittens and puppies. "You're sewing for Lissa and Jason's baby."

Mandy gave her a broad smile. "I want to be ready for this little girl."

"Now that they know they're having a girl, they can settle on a name, and you can make clothes."

"I'll have such fun with this little darling. If God hadn't brought Lissa here, I wouldn't have the joy of being close to a great-grandchild."

"The baby is blessed to grow up knowing her great-grandmother. Not everyone gets that opportunity."

With enthusiasm bubbling over, Mandy asked, "Do you want to look at the patterns with me? I hardly know what to make first."

They spent the next half-hour with their heads bent together. Though Stephanie knew nothing about sewing, Mandy's enthusiasm was contagious, and she was eager to see the tiny outfits when they were sewn.

"I suppose we should have lunch," Mandy said at last.

They went to the kitchen for ham sandwiches and tea. "Now I'll have to think of one hundred ways to use left-over ham," Mandy joked.

"You left some behind with Lissa. You might want to share those recipes with her."

"Lissa has never been one for cooking. I'm going to make up a couple of dozen frozen meals for them to use when the baby is born. It's a hectic time for new mothers to try to cook."

"She'll appreciate that."

Mandy nodded. "So will her mom. She'll want to come out for a while. She doesn't like to cook, either."

Stephanie lifted a brow. "I see why they were sad when you moved here from Houston. They missed your cooking."

Mandy chuckled. "I think you're right."

Stephanie's phone rang as they finished their lunch. The caller ID identified Alex. Stephanie's heartbeat quickened. What could he want? There was only one way to find out.

She answered. "Hi, Alex. How's your morning going?"

"It's been fine. I have an idea I want to bounce off of you. I know it's your day off and I shouldn't be bothering you, but I'd like your opinion."

"If you need me, I can come in," she said.

Alex hesitated. He wanted to tell her he needed her in his life all the time, not just at work. What would she say?

He cleared his throat "I was looking at your mix of green and rainbow colors on the slope and decided to plant cedar along the edge of the grass, instead of using bark mulch. What do you think?"

CHAPTER TWENTY

STEPHANIE CONSIDERED the idea, picturing it in her mind. "It would be less trouble in the long run. Landscape fabric eventually breaks break down. Dirt blows between the bark and then weeds grow. Of course, cedar would take upkeep, too. It always needs to be trimmed back or it takes over."

Chuckling, Alex said, "It's in their budget to have it trimmed."

She imagined the bottom rectangle of the yard. "I'm getting the picture in my mind. I think it might be pretty to have the cedar in splays spaced along the outer edge with bark in front and around it."

"Yes. I've seen that done. I'll give it thought and do a layout."

"I really could come in to help."

"No. I don't have a sitter for Daniel and it's your day off. I just needed to bounce my idea off of you. I'll let you get back to whatever you were doing."

"Nothing important. I've been rattling around. Mandy does so much, I have time on my hands. I'm not used to that."

"Then, it's probably good for you," he said, voice gentle. "I'll see you on Monday."

"Before then, unless you won't be at church."

"I plan to come. I'll see you there, then."

"The spring Bible study series is beginning this week. It sounds like it will be really good."

"I look forward to it. I've been getting a lot out of the lessons," he said.

He'd been longing to be closer to God. Ever since Kelly died, he'd distanced himself, not believing God cared as much about him as other folks. How could God allow those who loved and followed Him to suffer such loss? God could have prevented the accident that took Kelly. They would still be together as they should have been.

Deep in the recesses of his faith, he had never rejected the knowledge that God allowed painful things to happen to the people He loved. They might never know the reason for it in this life.

He put thoughts of the past out of his mind and attempted to concentrate on the loose ends of the project. As usual, Stephanie's suggestion worked beautifully.

He couldn't wait until Monday when he could show it to her. The weekend stretched interminably for Alex, and Sunday morning seemed a long way off.

In the afternoon, clouds darkened until they dumped two inches of snow.

Daniel grew restless. "Outside?" he asked, watching snow stick in the yard.

"It's cold and wet. You wouldn't like it."

Daniel's blue eyes pleaded. "Touch snow?"

Alex realized it was the concern for his comfort rather than Daniel's that held him in the warm house. He smiled at his small son. "It won't hurt you to get a little wet. Let's put your coat on. Every little kid should get to feel snow."

As soon as he was bundled, they walked onto the front porch. Daniel squirmed to get down. Alex set him on the front walkway, and he trudged off into the fluffy white powder. He kicked the snow and laughed as it scattered and settled again like a snowstorm above a tiny town.

After ten minutes of wandering through the enchanted playland, discomfort took its toll. Daniel raised his arms to be held. Shivering in his father's grasp, he didn't complain when they headed inside.

"Let's make hot cocoa and warm you up."

While the water heated, Alex peeled off Daniel's wet boots and gloves and got him dry socks. He set him in a kitchen chair beside the bay window, and they watched the snow fall as they enjoyed the warm drink. Afterward, he bundled him up for a nap and began clean-up chores around the house.

He wondered what Stephanie was doing. Maybe she was sitting and chatting with Mandy. He wondered if she were thinking about him. He wished they could work together. Even mopping the kitchen floor would be more fun if she were loading dishes nearby.

They would spend tomorrow morning together at church. Next week they would work side-by-side. The next holiday was Memorial Day. Perhaps he could arrange a barbecue. This brought another question to his mind. Should he buy Stephanie a croquet set so they could all play?

The clouds broke early in the evening, parting like curtains to show stars decorating the sky. Alex cleaned up their simple supper of eggs and bacon before stepping onto the front porch to admire the shallow blanket of snow glittering in the moonlight. Though some roads would be slippery that evening, they would be safe tomorrow since only a light freeze was predicted overnight. He was determined to make it to church tomorrow.

He prepared for bed, still debating about getting a croquet set for Stephanie. Just then, another idea struck him. Her birthday was two weeks away, in the middle of April. She'd mentioned wanting to see a movie coming out in a few days.

He could give her two tickets and hope she would invite him. More likely, she would ask Mandy, unless she remembered he'd told her he wanted to see it, too. In truth, he looked forward to being with her much more than seeing the film.

The next morning, Alex dressed Daniel in slacks and a cardigan. He looked more like a little boy than a baby. As he scooped him up and headed to the car, he wondered where the time had gone since he'd walked a colicky baby all through the night.

He looked for Mandy and Stephanie after he left Daniel in the nursery. He found them already seated in the third row on the right. Stephanie patted the seat beside her and smiled. "Saved just for you."

Sliding in beside her, he tried to concentrate on the greeting and opening hymn. The scent of lavender shampoo drifted from Stephanie's hair. It was intoxicating. Nonetheless, he forced his attention to the service. The pastor spoke about accepting forgiveness from God and extending it to others. He then got to the hard part, how to be the one to forgive and pardon.

How many grudges did he carry from his past? He hadn't thought about the cost. He'd blamed the driver who'd hit Kelly, even though it was ruled an unavoidable accident. It was time to focus on the pain the man must have felt as well as Alex's own loss. For the first time, he prayed for the driver with an honest desire for him to experience release for any guilt he might still feel.

At the end of the service, he walked out feeling like a weight had lifted from his chest. He wondered if it showed on his face.

Stephanie walked with him to the classroom. Inside, he experienced warm greetings from everyone there. The love and acceptance made him wonder why he'd avoided the fellowship after the accident. He enjoyed it now with Stephanie as well as the rest of the class.

When the class ended, Mandy insisted he and Daniel join them for lunch. "I figured you might put the box of seasonal decorations back in the attic for me. I don't want Stephanie falling just when her ankle's getting better."

"Neither do I. She might take time off work, and I need her there."

Stephanie drew her brows together into a frown. "Hey. I've managed to hobble around the office. I'm sure I could do it again unless I hurt the other ankle. That might be a little harder."

"Let's not chance it," Mandy said.

"I'll watch Daniel while you're up there," Stephanie told Alex. "I think Mandy has a picture book he'd like."

While Alex carried the box up, she entertained Daniel with the story of a puppy that got lost. By the time Mandy set food on the table, the puppy found his way home. The scent of tomato soup and grilled cheese sandwiches made Stephanie's stomach grumble with hunger.

She'd had only coffee and a piece of toast for breakfast. Though the Bible study class had doughnuts, she'd opted out, preferring to save her appetite for Mandy's lunch.

Alex came back down without incident. Daniel chatted happily as he nibbled his sandwich and slurped soup. Stephanie didn't understand much of what he said. Yet, she got the idea he was hoping for another egg hunt.

After lunch, Alex settled on the sofa with Mandy and said, "I saw lots of gladiola bulbs when I got a box from the garage to carry the Easter food."

She nodded. "They're very special to me. I've had them for years. I lift them out every winter."

"Someday, you'll have some for your great-granddaughters," Stephanie told her.

"Yes, I will. I hope they love them as much as I do. I'm going to separate them and line them in the garden along the back of the house. I also have iris I want to separate and spread out in the gardens on each side of the yard."

Alex cocked his head. "I'm sure the results will be amazing. Still, it's a lot of work. I'd be happy to lend a hand. Daniel and I could help you. Well, at least I could help you. Daniel could play in the yard."

Mandy patted his hand. "That's very kind, but you must have a lot to do at your house, what with a little boy and taking care of the house and your yard."

He grinned at her. "I could take payment in food if you'd make us lunch. I'm visiting my mother Saturday through Tuesday over Mother's Day. How about the next Saturday?"

"I'd love it," Mandy admitted. "Your timing would be perfect. I'll be spending Wednesday through Monday of that week with my great-granddaughter in Houston. Claire's great about sending pictures. Yet I'm sure baby Chelsea will be even more beautiful in person."

"When you get back you can watch Daniel while Alex and I can plant the garden," Stephanie said. "My ankle is almost healed. It will be fine by then."

Mandy's smile lit the room. "You're both spoiling me. My knees don't like gardening as much as they used to. What more could I ask than two professionals arranging my flower beds?"

Stephanie already looked forward to the job. She would spend an entire morning with her hands in the dirt and she would be doing it with Alex. The relaxed atmosphere of the garden would be a good setting to get to know each other better.

She turned her attention to what Alex was saying. "I hope Daniel remembers my parents this year. Memories are important. Sometimes it's all we have."

Mandy patted his hand again. "Don't worry, dear. He will."

The wistful tone left Stephanie to assume he spoke of Kelly. She knew holidays were challenging time for missing loved ones. She sent a silent prayer that Alex and Daniel would find comfort and could move past their loss.

Mandy changed the subject. "I'm going to bake cookies before I go. I'll pack some and leave some."

"If you make too many, Daniel and I can help you get rid of them," Alex offered.

"I always make too many," Mandy said.

Mandy smoothed Daniel's hair as he came over to sit on her lap.

Stephanie loved Mandy's cookies. "I won't have to cook. I'll have cookies for dinner."

"Oh no, you won't. I'll have food frozen for the days I'll be gone."

Becoming serious, Stephanie said, "That's too much work. I had to feed myself when I had an apartment. I can do it while you're gone. I can prove to myself I'm not completely spoiled."

"How about we share our food?" Alex suggested. "Daniel and I come for Mandy's good food one night and I buy take-out for the next."

Mandy's reply was fast. "That's a wonderful idea. You can all have dinner Wednesday through Friday when I'm away and Alex is still here. That way Stephanie won't get lonely."

Her suggestion was blatantly obvious as a matchmaker. Stephanie felt her cheeks heating. She hoped Alex didn't think any of this was her idea.

"On Saturday, when we're both gone, you could spend the evening with Linda and Tom. I'm sure they'd be glad for you to come," Alex told Stephanie.

Biting her lip, Stephanie wasn't sure how to answer. She hadn't been on the best terms with Linda. The last thing she wanted was to be an uncomfortable guest who had been imposed on her hostess.

"Please don't ask her to invite me. I'm happy just being here at the house," Stephanie said.

"All right. I know she'd feel bad if she found out you were alone on Mother's Day weekend. I'll feel bad, too," Mandy said.

"I'll be fine! I'll call my mom and then have a chance to do something unselfish. I'll serve Mother's Day dinner at a homeless shelter. The church is looking for volunteers."

"That's very kind of you to serve at the shelter. Still, it won't take all day," Alex said.

"Just promise you won't ask Linda, please," Stephanie said.

Though he scrutinized her closely, Alex said, "I won't ask her. You'll probably be tired from the workweek by Saturday. You'll be plenty busy."

The way he said it raised her suspicions. Was there a new landscape job in the works?

"What's that supposed to mean?" she asked.

Instead of an answer, he smiled at her. "You'll see."

CHAPTER TWENTY-ONE

AFTER A BUSY TWO WEEKS in which they completed the Pratt's project, Stephanie got home from work to find that she had received a small box in the mail from her parents. It would be her birthday gift, and whatever was inside would be a wonderful surprise.

When they'd asked what she wanted, she'd said she had everything she needed and really couldn't think of anything. When her mom didn't press her, she supposed they already had something in mind.

Mandy waited expectantly from her seat on the cushioned armchair for Stephanie to open it. "It's a birthday gift from your parents, isn't it?" she asked.

Stephanie nodded. "I don't know what it could be."

"Do you mind if I watch?"

"Of course not. From the size of the box, it's not the new bike I wanted as a kid."

Mandy grinned at her. "I've got a dusty old bike in the garage. Help yourself."

"Thanks. I'm more of a jogger now. What I need is a little dog to come with me."

"You like dogs, huh?"

Stephanie nodded. "I do. I've wanted one for the last several years. I've not lived in any place where I could have one."

"What kind would you get?" Mandy asked.

"I wouldn't care. I'd like a small or medium dog of any breed."

She peeled the tape from the box and pulled out a smaller box wrapped in birthday paper. When she got it open she discovered a new watch. She held it up for Mandy to see.

"It's so pretty, delicate, and feminine," Mandy said.

"I know. It's beautiful," Stephanie said. "I always get the cheap fifteen-dollar ones at a discount store. I hope I don't break it. I'm not the most coordinated person in the world. Maybe I'll only wear it on Sundays."

"I imagine your parents want you to enjoy it. They would want you to wear it every day."

"You're right. I will. I'm going to go call my parents and tell them how much I like it."

"Before you go, can you tell me if you have any plans for your birthday tomorrow? You know I plan to make you a cake." Mandy said.

"I have no plans and I think it's sweet of you to make me a cake. You mentioned German chocolate."

"You said it is your favorite."

"Oh, it is, though I don't think you could make a cake I wouldn't love," Stephanie said.

Stephanie was touched by Mandy's determination to make sure she had a good birthday. If she were alone in an apartment, tomorrow would be a lonely time. Her thoughts drifted to Alex. Would he remember tomorrow was her birthday?

IT SEEMED A GIFT FROM God that her birthday dawned with a sapphire sky and a warm spring breeze. Her phone buzzed and she read a text from her parents wishing her a happy birthday and promising to call when she got home from work.

She smiled as she read the text. Most of her birthday celebrations while she was growing up were jumbled in her memory. When she was small, there were birthday parties with her friends.

Later, there were family parties. Grandma had been with them then and had taken over baking the birthday cake.

When nostalgia threatened to overwhelm her, Stephanie shook off the past. The scent of the Hawaiian blend coffee drew her to the kitchen. She greeted Mandy, who was busy scrambling eggs. The toast popped from the toaster on the counter next to the stove.

"The toast is for you, dear," Mandy said. "I almost have eggs ready. I can't send you to work on your birthday without a good breakfast."

"Thank you! Birthday breakfast was always a tradition in my family. You make me feel at home," Stephanie said.

"This is your home. We share it, remember?" Mandy said.

Stephanie poured a cup of coffee. "I have the kindest roommate ever."

Mandy smiled as she slid scrambled eggs onto a plate. "We do get along well, don't we?"

"Yes, we do." Stephanie accepted the eggs and a slice of buttered toast.

They discussed their plans for the day while they sipped the thick brew and ate their eggs and toast. Stephanie noticed her lunch tote on the counter and supposed Mandy had packed her a lunch.

When she got to work, both Linda and Alex wished her a happy birthday. It would be nice to have someone take her out to celebrate. When she was engaged, Neal had taken her to a nice restaurant, not that she missed Neal very much. He was not husband material.

Alex interrupted her thoughts. "Do you have any special plans for tonight?"

"No. I'm staying home. Mandy is making German Chocolate cake. Maybe we'll watch a movie."

A grin spread across Alex's handsome face. "That sounds like fun. Cake and a movie say party to me."

She held out her wrist. "My parents sent me this watch. It will look more impressive to our clients than the cheap discount one I usually wear."

He held her wrist with his warm hand to get a better look, and goosebumps ran up her arm. What was wrong with her? He was only showing friendly interest. However, his touch felt personal and electrifying.

"I never noticed whether or not your old watch was classy, but this one is nice," he said.

"I only hope I don't break it. I stuck my arm in water with one of my last watches. It didn't survive." She tried to ignore the warmth in her cheeks from his touch.

"I'm sure they want you to wear it and enjoy it no matter how long it lasts."

She nodded. "That's what Mandy said, too. So, I'm going to wear it."

Changing the course of the conversation, she asked, "What do you want me to deal with first today? I could check on the mall job or I could touch base with our client in Colorado to tell him we're backed up, but I'm starting on the sketch."

"Check on the mall first. I want to make sure they are laying the sidewalk. If not, we're going to get behind. They should have the grass in, also."

"Okay. I'll get right on it."

ON THE DRIVE TO THE mall, she tried to keep mind on her job. Yet, a nagging sense of disappointment plagued her. Since Alex hadn't forgotten her birthday, she thought he might invite her to lunch. She would have treasured a card. She hadn't expected a present. Apparently, birthday wishes were all he had in mind.

She realized with chagrin the way she'd shown him her watch might have sounded like a hint. He might think a present would be too personal. Nonetheless, couldn't he have given her a card?

ALEX LOOKED OVER DESIGNS for the work that remained on the mall grounds. It was going well, and it looked as though they would meet the deadline for finishing. Since they were allowed to place their business sign at the project, he'd be surprised if they didn't get several new customers.

Stephanie kept creeping back into his thoughts. He had a hard time keeping his mind on the numbers when he checked the costs and expenditures for the job. She had no idea what was in store. It was going to be fun to see her surprise. Mandy was in on it, as were Linda, Lissa, and Jason. He couldn't wait to see the look on Stephanie's sweet face when she saw her present.

Thinking of her face was dangerous territory. He remembered the curve of her lips and that they were delicate and finely shaped. They would be so soft and intoxicating to kiss.

He chastised himself and was determined to keep his mind on the job. He didn't know if she would want him to kiss her. She'd never teased him the way some women did when they wanted a man's attention. Then again, he didn't think that would be Stephanie's way of attracting a man. Her sweet disposition and clever competence were far more tempting.

DURING HER LUNCH BREAK, Stephanie had a jog before eating the food Mandy had packed. Inside the lunch tote, Stephanie found a sweet card wishing her a happy birthday. She would be sure to thank Mandy for the lunch and the card.

Mandy reminded Stephanie of her grandmother. They had been close, and Grandma had made all of Stephanie's special occasions memorable. They had been best friends, and she still missed her grandmother. They had done a lot of gardening together. It was probably the main reason Stephanie loved plants as much as she did.

She sighed as she finished her lunch and packed it away. Grandma wouldn't want her to be sad on her birthday. God had blessed her with a beautiful day. The sun warmed the cool spring air and birds sang a happy chorus to her from the grove of trees that shaded the park. In the distance, she heard the roar of a lawnmower. Someone was getting an early start on mowing the grass.

She tossed her trash and set off across the park and through the neighborhood to arrive back at the office. During the afternoon, nothing else was said about her birthday. She felt childish in wishing Alex would make more of the occasion.

She thought of all the special things she would want to do for him on his big day, including a card, cookies, and a plaque for his parking spot that said, "King of the Hill" that was decorated with a grassy knoll speckled with wildflowers. She had already bought it, planning to save it for his birthday. Would it be awkward giving it to him now since he'd not given her anything?

When it was time to go home, she forced a light tone when she told Alex goodbye for the day. He hardly looked up as he replied in kind. With hurt feelings, she plodded to the car. He could have at least wished her a good birthday evening. She would have done that, and more, for him.

As she slid into the car, her phone alerted her to a text. She checked it to discover Mandy needed her to stop at the store for ice cream. Stephanie frowned. Wasn't German Chocolate cake sweet enough? She hoped Mandy wasn't asking for the ice cream because she thought Stephanie expected it. Nonetheless, she would stop and get it because Mandy had asked her to do so.

She arrived at the store and scrutinized the flavors. What would Mandy want? If she asked, Mandy would probably tell her to get what she liked best. Chocolate chip cookie dough ice cream won out and

Stephanie waited at the check-out while customers with carts full of groceries made their purchases.

Grouchiness threatened to ruin her mood. She reminded herself that Mandy had gone to the trouble to make her a cake and meal and this was a small thing to ask in return. By the time she checked out, she was anticipating arriving home to the heady scent of chicken fried steak with mashed potatoes and green beans. Her stomach rumbled at the thought.

After she parked in the driveway, she clutched the bag with the ice cream and headed toward the front door. With her key in hand, she unlocked it, stepped into the foyer, and froze.

A mass of voices shouted. "Surprise!"

She glanced at the faces and saw Lissa and Jason, Mandy, Linda and her family, and Alex and Daniel.

All she could stutter was, "Oh."

Daniel clapped his little hands and continued to shout. "Surprise!"

When Alex got him quiet, Mandy hugged Stephanie and asked, "Are you surprised?"

Stephanie nodded. "I never expected this! Alex and Linda never let on there was anything planned. Neither did you."

"That's the way it's supposed to work."

Mandy relieved her of the bag with the ice cream. "Let me put this in the freezer for you."

"Thanks. This was just so nice of everyone."

Lissa wore a broad grin. "We have a little surprise for you."

"Really? More?" Her curiosity piqued. "I can't imagine what it could be."

"You'll see."

Linda and Tom's kids clapped their hands over their mouths and stared at her with shining eyes. Baffled, Stephanie wondered what present for her would get the kids excited. She supposed they were swept up in the party mood.

She glanced around and noticed Alex and Daniel had disappeared. Maybe the surprise was in the kitchen. Perhaps they'd gotten her flowers.

She was still musing about it when Alex and Daniel came out leading the cutest dog she'd ever seen. Short black ears bent forward, and a white bandana of fur lay around its neck. She opened her mouth to ask Alex if he'd gotten Daniel a dog when Alex held the leash out to her, and realization dawned.

"We thought it was time you got your dog," Alex said.

She squatted down and petted him, and his tail began to wag. "He's for me?" she asked incredulously.

Alex nodded. "He's yours if you want him. Mandy told me you've wanted a dog for a long time, yet you couldn't keep one in your apartments. Mandy said she would be glad to have one here. He's a year and a half old and housebroken."

Stephanie called the dog over to her. "Come here, you gorgeous boy."

Without hesitating, the dog ran over and let her stroke his silky head. Stephanie cuddled the warm furry body, and he licked her chin.

"Where did you get him?"

"He's a rescue dog from the pound," Mandy said. "Do you like him?"

"I love him. What breed is he?"

The dog stared at Stephanie with brown eyes that were limpid pools of affection.

"What breed is he?" she asked.

"He's mostly Border Collie. They're a smart breed of herding dogs," Alex answered.

"What's his name?" Stephanie asked.

Alex chuckled. "His former owner called him 'Hatch' because he's a smart dog and is always hatching a plan to sneak food or to escape and roam the neighborhood. I'm sure you can rename him if you like. Was it okay to get him for you?"

Stephanie felt her eyes fill with tears. "Okay? It's wonderful! I love him. I want him if it's all right for him to be here."

She met Mandy's smiling gaze and asked, "Are you sure you don't mind?"

"Not a bit. I like dogs and he'll be good company while you're at work."

"Thank you." Stephanie buried her face in the soft fur while Hatch licked her arm.

Linda's children, Sarah, and Allen, edged closer. Daniel toddled over. The kids wanted to pet Hatch.

"He's all right with kids, isn't he?" Stephanie asked Alex.

"Yep. He's great. Daniel's crawled all over him."

Stephanie looked on while the kids doted on him. Hatch wagged his tail and licked whoever he could reach. He appeared to be a friendly, well-adjusted dog.

"The young man who had owned him joined the army and was shipping out overseas. He couldn't find anyone to take Hatch," Alex said.

Stephanie sat beside Hatch and the kids, with her arms wrapped around her legs. "I hope Hatch doesn't miss his old owner too much."

Alex cocked his head. "If anyone can make him forget, it will be you."

She would forever carry the memory of the endearing look on his face when he said those words. He made her feel as though they were the only people in the room. She realized she was staring into his eyes and tore her gaze away. She hoped no one else had noticed her fascination with this man.

Mandy interjected a welcome distraction. "Supper is ready. We should eat before it gets cold. Hatch will still be here when we finish."

They all followed Mandy into the kitchen, where the scent of chicken fried steak filled the air. The window above the sink was open, allowing a mellow breeze to ruffle the curtains. The sound of birds singing their evening songs made Stephanie forget any care she'd ever had.

After a prayer of thanksgiving by Tom, they filled their plates with Mandy's steak and fresh green beans. When complimented about the food, Mandy was quick to share the credit. "Lissa brought the mashed potatoes and Linda brought the rolls."

Stephanie scanned the faces of her friends and knew she was truly blessed. Instead of being alone, God had filled her life with friends who loved her. She and Alex had a good working relationship. Would there ever be more?

The three-tier cake sat atop a cake plate on the counter. Coconut peeked from the chocolate icing from the edges and on top of the cake. Stephanie knew from experience that Mandy's desserts would compete with any from the finest restaurants. As she filled up on the meat and potatoes, Stephanie saved room for the cake.

She blushed when they sang "Happy Birthday" to her and blew out the fancy unfolding flower candle Mandy had put on the cake. Mandy and Lissa cut the servings and Tom and Jason requested ice cream.

"Seriously?" Lissa said. "How can you two have that much sweet stuff?"

"Because we love it," Tom answered. "Besides, this is a special occasion."

Lissa rolled her eyes as Mandy scooped ice cream onto their plates. Linda's kids pushed their plates over for ice cream, too.

"Only one scoop each," Linda said.

"That was delicious. Thanks so much," Stephanie told Mandy.

"We're not done yet," Lissa said. "The dog was from Alex and Daniel. Jason and I went in with Linda's family and Mandy for a gift."

"This is too much," Stephanie said.

"Nonsense. We wanted to," Lissa said.

Linda and Tom pulled out a large package in birthday balloon wrap. Everyone gathered around while Stephanie sat on the floor to open it. Drawn like flies to honey, the kids settled next to her. Daniel reached for the package.

"Not yours, Daniel," Alex said. "Let Stephanie open it."

Daniel's expression drew into a frown.

"I don't mind help, if it's okay with you," Stephanie told Alex.

He nodded. "All right."

"Let's do it on three," Stephanie told the kids. "I'll count, and on three, we'll tear off the paper."

Six eager little hands poised above the present. When Stephanie reached three everyone tore into the wrap. Underneath the paper, they saw a soft kennel for Hatch. Inside the kennel, Stephanie found a leash, two dog dishes, and a bag of dog food.

Stephanie turned to the adults sitting on the couch and chairs. "Thank you all so much! Now I have everything I need for him."

Mandy said, "Since he's used to sleeping in a kennel, his owner dropped his old one off at the shelter when he brought Hatch.in. It was old and worn, so we thought he should have a new one."

"You are all so wonderful. I can't thank you enough," Stephanie said.

Linda chuckled. "I think you just did."

A short while later, everyone went home, leaving Stephanie alone with Mandy and Hatch. Hatch settled happily on the living room carpet while Stephanie and Mandy lingered over cups of decaffeinated coffee.

"Were you surprised?" Mandy asked.

"I was shocked! I didn't realize you zeroed in on my longing for a dog."

"I didn't think to get you one. I was telling Alex about how lonely you'd been in apartments and how you wished you'd had a dog. He took it from there. He's such a thoughtful man."

She studied Stephanie, as though waiting for validation. Stephanie would happily have prattled on for an hour about how much she liked Alex and how attractive she found him. However, if she confided her innermost thoughts, would Mandy take it as a hint step up her matchmaking? Stephanie would never want Alex to be pressured into dating her.

"He is thoughtful," she agreed.

She hurriedly changed the subject to rules about Hatch. "I'll be sure Hatch stays off your furniture and gets rid of any bad habits, like bothering your garden or digging."

"I don't want you to worry about him. Just enjoy him," Mandy said.

Stephanie smiled at her. "I will."

A little while later, after talking to her parents and telling them about Hatch, she and Hatch bedded down. He went happily into his kennel and didn't make a sound all night. Stephanie wished her night could have been as peaceful.

She was plagued by bad dreams about Alex accusing her of trying to take Kelly's place. No matter how much she protested, he insisted she was trying to worm her way into his heart and business. She awoke in a cold sweat early in the morning and could never get back to sleep.

Despite the dream, work went smoothly for the next few weeks. She settled into a routine of jogging with Hatch early each morning before she had to go to work, instead of jogging at the park. Since his business was brisk, Alex hadn't asked her to go there again. He ate lunch with Daniel and got right back to work. Stephanie worked over lunchtime and enjoyed the extra progress she made with her designs.

When the week of Mother's Day came, Mandy was in a dither to get packed and on the plane to see her granddaughter's baby in Houston. Since Stephanie usually worked during her lunch breaks, she didn't feel guilty about taking part of her morning off to drive Grandma Mandy to the airport in Durango. It was only an hour north of Farmington and Alex assured her he didn't mind.

She told him, "I'll combine it with business. I have an appointment to meet with the mall manager at ten o'clock."

"Are we on for supper Wednesday night?" he'd asked. "You promised we'd share meals until I have to leave."

"Of course. Mandy froze luscious lasagna. I can have it heated by six-thirty. Is that too late for Daniel to eat?"

"No. I'll ask the sitter to give him a snack at about four o'clock. That should hold him until supper is ready."

ON WEDNESDAY MORNING, Mandy got on the plane without a hitch. After she met with the mall owner, Stephanie headed back to Farmington. Alex dominated her thoughts. She was looking forward to their evening together. She hoped he felt eager to spend time outside of the office with her, too. He often complimented her on her talent. More than once, she'd caught him watching her when she looked up from her computer. Though she didn't dare to ask him, she would give more than a penny for his thoughts.

ALL DANIEL TALKED ABOUT on the way to see Stephanie for supper was the dog. When Daniel got older, Alex planned to get him a dog. He hadn't decided on a breed. For now, all he could think about was Hatch. He imagined Daniel in his backyard romping with the Border Collie. He reminded himself that Hatch belonged to Stephanie. If Hatch lived at his house, so would Stephanie. He realized he was smiling.

When they knocked on the door, Hatch barked a greeting. Stephanie met them with a smile and Daniel immediately went for the dog. He sat on the floor in the living room beside Hatch and began to pet him. He cooed in baby language and Hatch wagged his tail.

Stephanie and Alex were left facing each other. For a moment, he felt awkward. With Daniel occupied with the dog, it felt as though they were alone. Every instinct told him to give her a hug and maybe a kiss on the cheek, though he longed to kiss her lips. Yet, he didn't dare jeopardize their working relationship.

His chance was lost as Stephanie said, "Come on into the kitchen. Our food is done."

He followed behind her. The meal smelled delicious as it heated in the oven. When Stephanie set it on two hot pads, he noticed it was a big pan and would be enough for leftovers tomorrow. He planned to ask for some for lunch.

"I was going to tell you we got the payment for the Johnson job you handled. They were happy with your ideas for the slope," he said.

"The ideas were yours, too," she said.

"Right. But since we got paid for it today, I have a little something for you."

He extended an envelope. She took it, wondering what he could have for her. She opened it and pulled out a check for five hundred dollars. Staring at it, she asked, "You pay me a salary. What's this for?"

"It's a bonus. I've had the best year ever. A lot of it was due to you. Now, I'm asking you to hold things down while I go out of town. You deserve something extra for that."

"Thank you! I appreciate it. I'll have to think about what to do with it."

He smiled. "If you're like me, you won't have a problem finding something to spend it on."

"I'm sure I won't Thank you, again. I wanted to tell you the last shrubs arrived for the Colorado mall job. The owners are happy with how it's been going. I've projected completion by the end of the month."

"That's great. We may have a few delays due to the rain projected this week, but we'll be okay if it runs a few days over."

She frowned. "I hope not. That cuts the profit."

"Nothing we can do about the weather."

She nodded. "We'll hope for the best."

"I have to do some shopping tomorrow for Mother's Day. Linda is keeping Daniel while I go. Is there anything I can pick up for you?"

"A new toaster for Mandy. Hers is ancient and not working very well. The toast pops up three times before it's finally crisp, even on the hottest setting."

"I can do that. Anything else?"

She shook her head. "I shopped online for my mom. It should arrive by Friday."

"You're lucky to be finished already. I don't have any ideas."

"Would her mom like a gift certificate to a restaurant? Your parents could have a night out."

He brightened. "That's great. I know where they like to eat. You just saved me a long evening of shopping. It just takes a minute to pick up a toaster."

He touched her gently on the cheek. "You not only help with problems, but you're also great with gift ideas."

His enthusiastic compliment warmed her heart. To cover her fluster from the praise, she asked, "Are you going to church with your parents on Sunday?"

"I am. We'll be at the church where I grew up. It will be good, but I'll miss going with you and Mandy."

She would miss him, also. She wanted to walk in with him, to sit next to him and be with him while the sacred scripture was read, and the sermon given.

"I'll miss having both of you here," she said. "I'm glad you're taking Daniel to church while you're out of town. Someday, he'll grow into a Godly man like his father."

Alex gazed into her eyes. "Not Godly enough. I have a long way to go."

"We all do. Fortunately, God loves us, anyway."

Stephanie looked into his face and felt admiration for his faith and strength.

He changed her thoughts by asking, "Will you go to dinner with me tomorrow night? It's my turn to feed us and I don't feel like fast food."

Stephanie thought about Linda. What would Linda think if she heard about the meals they were having together? Would she decide Stephanie was luring him to get her hooks into the business?

Nonetheless, her heart won out. "Thanks. I'd like that."

His smile showed the dimple near his mouth. "Do you want to leave right after work? The sitter said she could watch Daniel until his bedtime."

"Sure. That's great."

It occurred to her he'd already planned it if he'd asked the sitter to watch Daniel during dinner. Did he crave her company the way she craved his? He was everything she wanted in a man. Could it be he felt the same about her or was it wishful thinking?

SHE DRESSED CAREFULLY for work the next morning in a red silk blouse and black slacks. She brushed her auburn hair until it rested in glossy waves on her shoulders. Then, with a little green eye shadow, she turned from the mirror, grabbed her purse, and headed out the door.

When she arrived at work, Alex looked at her and said, "I've never seen you look more lovely."

Though they discussed only business for the rest of the day, Stephanie couldn't take her mind off of the upcoming evening.

When they quit for the day, Stephanie loitered a bit, waiting for Linda to leave. If she knew Alex was taking her to dinner, it would raise more suspicion.

When Linda called to her a good night from the reception area, Stephanie turned off her computer and joined Alex, who'd been waiting for her in his office. They locked up and walked out together. Linda was pulling out of the lot into the street. Stephanie felt relieved that Linda wouldn't see them leave together.

"We can take my car and come back for yours after dinner," Alex suggested.

"That would be great. I don't know where we're going, anyhow."

He winked. "I think you'll like it."

He was handsome in a blue sports coat that made his eyes the color of a summer sky. Her pulse raced with eagerness to spend the evening with him. Her gaze went to his lips and her cheeks heated when he smiled. Did he know her guilty secret? She wanted him to kiss her. She'd fallen in love with her boss and feared he had only friendly concern for her. She had to get a hold of her thoughts before he noticed, and she made a fool of herself. Any longer, and he might read her thoughts and she could not be comfortable working beside him ever again.

Light spilled from the Italian restaurant as they parked in the lot. A pretty, dark-eyed hostess greeted them inside. She took Alex's name and told them it would be only a few minutes. As they waited, they admired the photos of Italy on the wall.

"Do you have any Italian in your bloodline?" Alex asked.

"Not that I know of. You?"

"Scottish, I believe."

"Are you the owner of a castle in the old country?"

He chuckled. "I wish. How about you? What's your heredity?"

Stephanie shrugged. "I have no idea."

The hostess seated them at a table near the window. Stephanie breathed a sigh of relaxation at the homey atmosphere. They dined on fettuccini and cheese ravioli and chatted about what drew them into the landscape business.

They talked about Alex's upcoming visit to his family. Stephanie wondered if she would meet his parents someday. They sounded wonderful. She imagined herself as part of his family. It was silly. She had no reason to expect it would ever happen.

As they finished the meal, Stephanie said, "I love Italian food."

"So do I, which is good since you sent me so much of the leftovers from last night," Alex said.

"Mandy didn't want us to go hungry. Tomorrow night we'll have chicken pot pie."

She stared across the table and realized she could never get tired of looking at this man. For a moment, she allowed herself to imagine being his wife and sitting across the breakfast table from him each morning. They could grow old together.

She became aware that Alex was watching her. Fortunately, he couldn't read her thoughts. Nonetheless, she felt embarrassed.

"You've gotten quiet. Is everything all right?" he asked.

She smiled. "Yes, perfect. I've had a fun evening."

"It doesn't have to end. The sitter said she'd put Daniel to bed. Do you want to see a movie?"

He surprised her by running a finger along her cheek. "I enjoy your company."

Her heartbeat tripled. "I'd love to see a movie."

Staring into his eyes, she longed to snuggle against him. What would it feel like to have his arms around her?

"I just happen to have the movies pulled up on my cell phone. You can choose whatever you'd like to see," he said.

She studied the ads. "This one looks good. Do you know anything about it?"

"I've heard it's exciting."

They sat shoulder to shoulder in the dark theater, jumping at each surprise and laughing at themselves. When it was over, they walked to the car with his arms around her shoulders. Her heart felt lighter than air. In one evening, their relationship had gone from covert to open interest in one another. She hoped it would grow like a rose, slowly unfolding into full bloom.

When he took her back to her car, he kissed her lightly on the lips before she got in. His touch lingered. It would seem forever until he got back from visiting his mom. With a deep sigh, she realized if they began dating, there would be no going back. They wouldn't be able to pretend there was nothing more between them than boss and employee. If the romance didn't work out, it might cost her the job. Did she want to take that chance?

She drove home and sat in the living room for the next hour listening to Christian music and wondering if she should hide her feelings from Alex. As she considered the pros and cons, her heart rebelled in giving up the chance to find the love of a lifetime. She loved her job and wanted to be around to see his company grow and thrive. If he did return her feelings and found out about her struggle with cancer, he might feel differently about her.

She retired at midnight and though she was tired from the expenditure of emotional energy, she knew the dilemma would probably keep her awake. As she lay in bed, she filled the time before sleep by praying for God's guidance in the relationship.

WHEN DANIEL WOKE THE next morning, Alex told him, "In two more days, you get to see Grandma and Grandpa. We're going to get on an airplane tomorrow and fly there. You've seen airplanes in the sky."

Daniel held his fingers an inch apart. "Little."

Alex chuckled. "Airplanes aren't little. They look small because they're so far away."

Daniel toddled off and reappeared with an eight-inch plastic plane. "This big," he said.

Alex laughed at the naivety of his small son.

"You'll find out," he told Daniel.

The next morning, Alex made eggs and toast. He let Daniel hold the plane while they ate. Alex's thoughts drifted to the dinner they would have with Stephanie tonight. He remembered the kiss from last night and longed to taste her soft lips again.

When he got to work, Linda asked, "Are you packed for your trip?"

He nodded. "I got that done yesterday. I hate being stressed at the last minute."

"Do you want to come for supper tonight?" Linda asked.

"Stephanie and I have been trading off with supper. Mandy had frozen meals and Stephanie is sharing them."

"That's nice, I suppose."

Her tone sounded dubious.

"Don't you like Stephanie?"

Linda sighed. "I suspect her motives. She's made herself invaluable, hasn't she? After the wonderful marriage you had with Kelly, I don't want to see you get stuck with someone who wants to control you and run your business. I'm not saying Stephanie has that motive, but it does worry me."

"I know her well enough to assure you she doesn't. So quit worrying. I'm a grown man and I'll be fine," Alex assured her.

She sighed and said, "Very well. I'll stop playing mother hen and stay out of it from now on. Tom keeps telling me it's your life. Why do I care who you date? Still, I don't want to see you get hurt."

"I appreciate that," Alex said. "But you'll see I'm right."

The day passed quickly. At work, Stephanie was completely professional with no hint that she had been affected by their more intimate time together. Before she left for the day, she told him she looked forward to seeing Daniel and him that evening. Did she only desire companionship to pass the time while Mandy was a

way, or was it more?

He felt nervous anticipation on the way to her house. Surely, she suspected he cared for her. Did she have feelings for him, too? He expected he would soon find out.

CHAPTER TWENTY-TWO

ALEX PULLED INTO THE driveway of Mandy's modest brick home and released Daniel from his car seat. The little boy had been chattering the whole way about riding on the airplane. He seemed to think Stephanie was coming with them, and Alex had been unable to convince him she was not going to come.

Alex let his imagination wander. If she were to come, she would meet his parents. They had been encouraging him to think about becoming more social, perhaps dating again. They would like Stephanie. She was thoughtful and industrious. She was also most attractive.

Stephanie opened the door before he had a chance to ring the bell. "I saw your lights in the driveway," she said.

Daniel reached for her, and she took him into her arms. "If you come this way you'll be rewarded," she said.

Alex followed her through the living room and into the kitchen where he inhaled the scent of chicken baked in rich gravy. He saw a side of cheesy scalloped potatoes sitting next to a bowl of green peas.

His stomach rumbled. "I didn't know I was so hungry until I got here."

"It's all compliments of Mandy. There's even cherry pie for dessert." Stephanie said.

His phone buzzed. He read the message and said, "It's from Linda. She has a question about rescheduling a client. It will just take me a moment to answer."

When he had replied to the text, Stephanie asked, "Does she know you're here tonight?"

He hesitated, and then said, "Yes. You know she's worried that you have motives of worming your way into a share of the company. She's coming around, though. She admitted she was over-protective. She and Kelly were close."

Stephanie sighed. "We talked. I can assure both of you that all I want is to do a good job of satisfying clients and growing your business."

Alex accepted a glass of iced tea. "You've done both very well and I appreciate your hard work."

Instead of replying, she turned her attention to Daniel. He had climbed into a chair and found a roll to munch on.

He grinned at her. "I hungry, Sefani. I eat this, and I get pie."

Raising a brow, she said, "I think you'll have to eat more than a roll."

Alex put his hand over Daniel's small one. "Wait until you get the rest of your food and we have prayed to eat the roll."

He told Stephanie, "Cherry pie is one of his favorite foods."

She smiled at Daniel. "I like cherry pie, too."

They dished out the dinner and Alex prayed over the food. After Stephanie added a prayer for their safe travel, they dug into the tasty dinner. Daniel ate the chicken and potatoes on his plate, yet balked at the peas.

"Eat them if you want pie," Alex told him.

Daniel scowled at the green balls as though they were his enemy. Finally, he gave in and put a spoonful in his mouth. After a second spoonful, Alex told him he could be done. Daniel looked as proud of his accomplishment as if he'd just won the Super Bowl.

Stephanie said, "My parents let me have ice cream when I ate my spinach. It almost wasn't worth it. When I grew up, I didn't touch it for years. Then, I discovered I liked fresh spinach in salads."

"Daniel's problem is his patience. He doesn't want to sit still long enough to eat. Then, he's hungry an hour later."

Daniel held out his plate to Alex. "I have pie?"

"Yes. You ate your supper."

He cut a small slice of cherry pie from the crusty delicacy on the counter.

Daniel dug in with gusto, managing to get more pie in his mouth than he did in his lap.

"I brought a puzzle to keep him busy when he finishes his pie. It's hard to talk with a two-year-old at the table," Alex said.

"He's awfully cute, though."

"Yes. He is!" Alex agreed.

As they lingered over dessert and coffee, they talked about their families, their upbringings, and their experiences in coming to know the Lord.

"We have a lot in common," Alex said.

"We do, though I've never experienced a loss as profound as yours," Stephanie said.

"It's been rough. For a long time, I didn't think I'd ever be truly happy again."

"Now you do?"

He gave her a long look that took her breath away. "Maybe."

She waited, hardly breathing, not knowing what to say.

His eyes held her gaze. He seemed to be framing his next words. When he spoke, it was with careful thought. "I was hoping we might spend more time together outside of work. I admire so many things about you. I want to get to know you better."

Stephanie could hardly believe she was hearing words she'd only dreamed that he'd say. She composed herself before answering. "I'd like that. As you said, we have a lot in common."

He pushed his empty plate away. "It's more than that, don't you think?"

She looked into his eyes and saw longing that pierced her heart. He wanted her to be with him, just as she had been hoping. She studied his handsome face. God had sent her to a man who needed her love, and she truly did love him.

She hesitated. Her pulse raced and she took a deep breath. "Yes. It is more than that!"

He touched her cheek lightly. "You rest while I get Daniel settled with a video on his iPad. I'll come back and help with the dishes, then."

She waited until he left with Daniel before she began to rinse, load the dishwasher, and put away the food. By the time he returned, she was nearly finished.

He shook his head. "I should have known. You wouldn't let work sit if you could be doing it. Let me wipe the table, and will you sit down with me then?

"Of course. Everything will be done."

A few moments later, they sat on the sofa with Daniel, who was engrossed in his cartoon dinosaur show. Alex took Stephanie's hand. "I don't want to presume you feel the way I do, but ever since our first picnic in the park, I've missed you when we weren't together. If you don't want to hear this, tell me now before I feel like a fool."

She drowned in the depth of his eyes, so full of hope. She'd fantasized about this moment. "If you're a fool, then so am I. But there's something I need to tell you."

She paused. Her heart thudded in her chest. She licked her lips, nervously. They were nearly too dry to speak. "Several years ago, I was diagnosed with cancer. I was treated, and the doctors believe I've been cured. My last check-up showed no sign of the disease. You deserve to know about it if we are thinking of pursuing a relationship."

For a moment, he didn't speak, leaving her to worry that he would decide not to risk his heart. He leaned forward and drew her to him and kissed her gently before saying, "I had a healthy wife who was taken from me in an instant. It made me realize nothing is certain in life. If the doctors believe you are cured, that's good enough for me."

Tears filled her eyes. "I was scared to tell you. I thought you might walk out."

"If you thought that, you have no idea how much you've come to mean to me. I've been praying I wasn't wrong about your feelings for me. I've been thinking about things we could do together when I get back from my trip. Do you like to go to another movie? "

"I'd like that."

She sat close to him with her head on his shoulder. The scent of his aftershave filled her senses as they chatted for another hour. Daniel became tired and cranky at that point and Alex and his son had to leave.

The picture of the dark-haired beauty lodged in Alex's mind as he drove home. She was not only beautiful, but she was smart. She'd proved that on the job, and her spunk and confidence impressed him. However, it was her sweet personality that had won his heart. He'd resisted his feelings for too long. Now he'd fallen in love and there was no turning back.

They would be apart next week when he and Daniel went back east to visit his folks. He usually looked forward to the trip. Now that he and Stephanie were getting along so well, he wished it could wait a while. Nonetheless, the tickets were bought, and the family was expecting them. Stephanie would be here when he returned. They could pick up where they left off. While he was away, he would remember her enchanting smile.

CHAPTER TWENTY-THREE

MONDAY MORNING, LINDA smiled at Stephanie when she walked into the lobby. She'd been friendlier in the last few weeks. Perhaps she'd finally decided Stephanie didn't want to take over the company, after all.

"I'm going to the new project off of Foothills Drive. I shouldn't be gone more than an hour," Stephanie said.

"I'll hold down the fort," Linda promised.

Stephanie checked her computer for messages and returned calls to two clients. A half-hour later, she was on the road to the job. The office complex they were landscaping was challenging. Rocks and dirt and a few piñon trees were the only foliage on the property. They had cleared it and put down xeriscaping. Yucca, sedum, and thyme were planned for beds beneath the Texas Ebony trees. There was still the walkway to the building to construct and planters to build.

She paused, imagining the completed project. Lavender, lamb's ear, and catmint might make good choices to plant near the building. Her afternoon would be consumed with this project.

She wandered the property, speaking to the workers and inspecting the work that had been done since her last visit. After giving the foreman a few additional suggestions, she returned to the office.

Her cell phone buzzed. The call was from Alex. "Hey, how's it going?" she asked.

"I'm glad to be off the plane. Daniel got bored on the second leg of the trip and wanted to go home. Now that we're here, he's being spoiled rotten and he's happy again."

"What about you? Are you having a good time?"

"Yeah, it's good to see my parents. My sister and her family are coming for dinner tonight."

"She'll love seeing Daniel."

"I know. He's the center of the universe here."

"A little extra attention won't hurt him," Stephanie said.

"I suppose not. How's your morning going?" he asked.

"I went to the project on Foothills. It looks good. I'm going to run some numbers on costs for the mall. The cold in late April slowed it down," she said.

"That always happens when we get freezes late in the year. They'll get back on track."

"I hope so." She didn't want to show she was nervous about the delay. They wouldn't get the next payment until the agreed-upon work was done. If Alex weren't worried, she would trust his judgment.

The conversation became personal when Alex voice got husky and he said, "I miss you a lot."

"I really miss you, too," she whispered.

They hung up and she got back to her projects, her mind on Alex as he dominated her thoughts..

She stayed busy visiting the landscape sites. Work would start again at the mall tomorrow and Mandy was due home tonight, which cheered her considerably.

Plans were in place for the crew to return to work in Colorado. Everything was looking up. Stephanie hummed as she finalized the plans for the office complex.

Later in the afternoon, a call came from the Colorado mall foreman. "We've got a problem."

Tension gripped her. "What is it?"

"The concrete on the walkway cracked. We're going to have to remove it and the sub-grade, compact it, and re-pour."

"Will that be expensive?"

"I'm afraid so. Now that the weather has warmed, we shouldn't have any problem with it setting."

"How long will it take to re-do the job?" Stephanie asked, her stomach clenching.

"About two weeks."

"That will put us behind schedule on finishing."

"It could, unless we can find a way to make up some time."

Heart racing, she stared out the window when they clicked off. The mall had been particular about the deadline. Even if the contractor who poured the concrete was at fault, they still wouldn't finish in time.

Her heart was heavy when she called Alex back.

"Hi, Stephanie, I still miss you! We've been having a wonderful time, though."

She bit her lip, hearing voices in the background. It was a happy time for him, being home with his family. She didn't want to spoil it.

"I'm glad you've had fun. However, I've got some bad news about the Colorado job. The cement didn't set right. It cracked. They have to dig it out and re-pour. I don't see any way we can make the deadline. I'm so sorry. I feel like this is all my fault."

The silence on the other end made her cringe. Was agreeing that she'd failed him?

At last, he spoke. "I'm going to have to get with our accountant to see what this means for us. We still have a contract with the mall."

Tears welled in her eyes. "I'm so sorry."

He sighed. "These things happen. We'll figure it out. Stay on the crew until I get back. I'll check the temperature for the day it was poured. The contractor may be at fault. For now, get our guys working on taking it out."

"I will. If it wasn't cured correctly, won't they have to do it over at their cost?"

"First, we must establish that's what happened. The sooner I get on it, the better. I'll start making calls."

"All right. See you soon."

She clicked off with a heavy heart. The end of his holiday was now ruined. Instead of enjoying his family, he would have to work. She rested her chin on her hands and asked God, "Lord, why did you let this happen? I'm in love with him but I've damaged his business. What if he can't forgive me?"

A few minutes later, Linda knocked on the door. "I just heard what happened. Our foreman contacted me to send out supplies to break concrete. Even if the company that poured the concrete is at fault and they must pay to do it over, aren't you behind on that job?"

Her face, pinched in a frown, only made Stephanie feel worse.

"Unfortunately, yes. We are behind," Stephanie answered.

Linda's frown deepened. "You have a contract with the mall to finish by the deadline. If you don't make it, they might not pay for the work that's been done. They could hire a different company to finish and leave Alex out all the money for this job. I don't have to tell you how bad that would be for our company."

Stephanie fought against the tears that threatened to spill over her cheeks. Linda suspected her of wanting to manage the business? This fiasco would only convince her that Stephanie had tried and done it poorly. If this turned out as badly as it seemed it would, Alex might not be able to forgive her. She would offer her resignation once she helped him regain financial stability, unless he wanted her gone sooner.

Forcing herself to look Linda in the eye, she said, "I feel terrible about it. Two weeks of cold put it off schedule and now the concrete is no good. I know it's a potential disaster for Alex. Trust me. I'll go quietly if he wants me to resign."

Linda's dumbstruck expression surprised her. "He doesn't want you to leave. That would be the worst thing you could do. I'm not blind. I know it's become personal between you two."

If Alex lost the company because of her, Stephanie wouldn't be able to stay. She choked on a bitter laugh. "I don't think he'll feel the same way about me."

Linda shook her head as Stephanie turned for the door. "I think he will."

Compelled to find the truth, Stephanie began researching the weather conditions on the day that the concrete was laid. It was below freezing. What was the process the contractor used for curing it?

She called their foreman. "Who was on the job the day the concrete was poured?"

A pause followed. "I don't recall. I can check the timesheets and get back to you."

"That would be great. I need to talk to them. Thanks." She hung up before the foreman could say another word.

A little later she got a call from one of the men. "I was in Colorado when the concrete was poured."

"How was it cured? "

"Insulting blankets were used. I worried about the ground being frozen hard, but no one else though it was a problem."

She ran a hand through her hair. "I'm going to call Alex to see what he's found out. Thanks for the information."

Alex sounded harried when he answered.

"Have you talked to the contractor yet?" she asked.

"He assures me the temperature was barely below freezing and that he used blankets."

Stephanie replied, "Our guy said the ground was definitely frozen. That's why it cracked. The contractor should pay to re-do it."

He sighed. "We can't prove he's at fault."

The lump in her throat nearly choked her. "Then you're stuck with the cost?"

"We'll talk when I get back. I'm going to speak to the mall about extending the deadline."

She needed to get off the phone before she broke into sobs. "All right. See you soon."

He hadn't asked her to talk to the mall owner. He didn't trust her to deal with the mess she'd gotten him into. Why should he?

Mandy arrived home that evening. It didn't take long for her to sense that Stephanie was deeply upset. Her hug brought Stephanie to tears. "I thought this job would open new doors for Alex. Instead, it's ruined him."

Mandy took her hands and sat with her on the couch. "Have you prayed about this? Maybe God has a solution."

Stephanie felt the burden heavy on her heart. "Do you think God has time for the mess I've made?"

"Of course. I'm going to ask for His help with this problem. Will you join me?"

They bowed their heads and prayed together.

Though Stephanie felt better, she didn't see a solution to the problem.

ALEX DEPLANED FROM his flight on Tuesday, weary and exhausted from reading and singing to Daniel for most of the trip. He hadn't yet decided what to do about the disaster at the mall. They'd set the date for the grand re-opening and the landscape wouldn't be ready on time.

He didn't want Stephanie to be devastated. It wasn't her fault. Still, he wished she hadn't talked him into taking the job.

He hadn't planned to come into the office until Thursday. With the problem at hand, he dropped Daniel at the sitter's and arrived at the building just before three o'clock.

Linda shot him a sympathetic look. "Any good news?"

"No. I spoke to the contractor. The temperature wasn't optimal, yet he said they took every precaution to prevent moisture. Our guys say they used insulating blankets. I'm not sure we have any recourse."

"You could take him to court," Linda suggested.

"It's too expensive. If we lost, we'd be finished."

"What are you going to do?"

He shook his head. "I can try for a small business loan."

"Tom and I have been praying for you and Stephanie. She feels terrible."

"I know. It's not her fault. I'm the one who okayed the project."

Linda cocked her head, studying him. "I've changed my mind about Stephanie. She plans to stay and do all she can to help sort this out and be sure you're solvent. Then, she said she will offer her resignation. It's you she loves, not your firm."

"We will get through this, all of us together, with God's help. I'm going to go ask Stephanie if she's come up with anything useful from the people she's talked to."

Linda nodded, turning back to her work as he walked down the hall to Stephanie's office.

Stephanie glanced up to see him in her doorway. Dark circles under her eyes led him to wonder if she'd gotten any sleep. It pained him to know she'd blamed herself for the disaster, for he was convinced her motives had been pure.

Her lips quivered in an uncertain smile. "I talked to the mall owner. He's going to speak to the board of directors to see if they'd be willing to delay the grand re-opening ceremonies. Our deadline is feasible if they give us two more months."

He wanted to wrap her in his arms. Yet he was unsure if that would be wise. If she blamed herself as much as he thought, she'd either pull away or burst into tears. Neither would help them solve the problem.

Instead, he strode in and sat in the chair opposite her desk. "That's the first encouraging thing that's happened since the weather slowed us down and the concrete cracked. I've thought a lot about this on the way back. I gave this company over to God. If He is for us, we'll get through this and stay solvent."

With a shuddered breath, she replied, "I hope so. You're kind not to fire me."

He longed to tell her the last thing he wanted was to fire her. He longed to marry her. That would have to wait, for now.

His cell rang. He saw it was the contractor.

"Yes, Dave?"

To his surprise, the man wanted to meet with him.

"I'm coming from a job in Farmington. How about if I stop by and we talk about the concrete?"

"Sure," Alex said. "I'm in the office. I'll wait for you."

When they clicked off, he told Stephanie what happened. "I guess we'll see where this goes," he said.

Dave arrived with raindrops beading on his leather jacket and jeans that covered his tall, lean form. He shook hands with Alex and Stephanie and accepted a cup of black coffee once he was seated in Alex's office. He brushed back a lock of black hair back from his damp forehead and said, "I thought this matter deserved immediate attention. My reputation is important to me, whether my crew was at fault or not. I'd like us to partner up again when you have other jobs in my area. So, here's what I'm offering. You chip out the concrete and I'll haul it away and re-pour. We can split the cost of materials."

Alex's brows went up. He nodded at Dave, barely able to speak.

"That's a fair offer. It's good to deal with a man with integrity. I expect it will take us a good week, maybe two, to be ready."

"Business is slower this time of year. Give me a couple of days' notice and I can send out a crew."

After finalizing a few more details, Dave left for home. Stephanie had not said a word during the meeting. Now, it came out in a flood.

"What a relief! It doesn't fix everything. But.it still cuts the expenses quite a bit."

He watched her features relax. She took a deep breath. He expected she'd been holding it for the last two days. He took her hands and drew her up to him. "As I said, this company is in God's hands, and so are we. Come over for supper tonight. Daniel would like to see you."

She snuggled close, laying her head on his shoulder. "Can I bring anything?"

"You can help carry in the pizza I'm ordering."

"With pleasure," she murmured.

Later, Linda called as they sat at the table sharing a hot pepperoni pizza. Alex drew his attention away from his beautiful Stephanie who held his son while they nibbled slices. Stephanie stopped eating.

Staring at him, he knew she guessed who was on the phone.

Linda was talking fast in her excitement. "I hope it's all right, but Tom told some of the guys at church about your problem. Several of them work construction and volunteered to come out to the project tomorrow to help clear out the cracked concrete. I figured you could use the help."

"Use the help?" he exclaimed. "I certainly could! I'll provide all the pizza they can eat when they're done."

"Great. Tom will call them back and let them know."

Gratitude bubbled in his chest at what God had done. Could either he or Stephanie ever doubt again that, within His will, God answers prayers?

"With all the help we'll have, we'll get the concrete out in a couple of days and meet the deadline. I don't think we'll be closing the doors of our company after all," he said.

She bit her lip, eyes filling with tears. "Our company?"

"It looks like everything is back on track. Will you marry me and help me run it? Will you be my partner in a forever life together, too?"

Spilling over, tears ran down her cheeks. "If you still trust me, I will marry you and do my best to further the business and I will love you forever."

He nodded at Daniel. "I come with a little boy, you know."

"I love you and your little boy. Stephanie said, her emotions spilling over with joy and gratitude to God..

He knelt and put his arms around the two loves of his life. Kissing her cheek, he said, "You've made me the happiest man on earth. I can't wait to begin our life together."

Get Book Three in this series JACK OF HEARTS.

Don't miss out!

Visit the website below and you can sign up to receive emails whenever Karen Cogan publishes a new book. There's no charge and no obligation.

https://books2read.com/r/B-A-QNTE-BIWAB

BOOKS 2 READ

Connecting independent readers to independent writers.

www.ingramcontent.com/pod-product-compliance
Lightning Source LLC
Chambersburg PA
CBHW072058170626
46813CB00004B/1404